DETOUR

Global Endeavor
PUBLISHING

ALSO BY PAUL B KOHLER

DETOUR

**BOOK TWO OF THE
HUMANITY'S EDGE TRILOGY**

Edited by Ellen Campbell and Allison Krupp
Cover design by Paul B. Kohler
Interior design and layout by Paul B. Kohler

ISBN-13: 978-1-940740-18-8
ISBN-10: 1-940740-18-5

www.paulkohler.net

Give feedback on the book at:
Amazon: amazon.com/author/paulkohler
info@paul-kohler.net
Twitter: @PaulBKohler
Facebook: facebook.com/Paul.B.Kohler.Author

Printed in the United States of America

First Edition

1.

I t rained most of the day before the storm pulled up anchor shortly after midnight, the welcomed deluge reducing to a mere drizzle just in time for Sam to start her shift.

"Jesus H. Christ!" she bellowed from the vacant observation tower perched some forty feet above the container yard. "How many times do I have to tell them?"

She was referring to the shift schedule hanging on the wall just inside the catwalk door. Printed in eighteen-point Comic Sans font, her name was spelled out. Samantha Anne Wells. Without batting an eye, she crossed out the "antha," those disdained extra syllables. Sam was the only name she'd gone by since she was a little girl. Samantha was only used by . . . well, her dad, and he'd passed away years ago.

Sam traced her finger across the schedule and found that not only did she have to work her third straight graveyard shift, she was scheduled for that same time slot every single day for the remainder of the week. To make matters worse, she was scheduled with Malcolm.

She shuddered, sensing his presence just outside the door. She'd heard him barking orders at one of the yard attendants just moments before, his voice sounding dog-like, ready to attack.

Just a few more weeks, Sam thought, and she could quit her lousy job for good. She'd have enough saved to visit her sister in New England, until she could figure out her next step. She hadn't been herself in years, she felt stretched thin, ragged. And she was only thirty-two years old.

She knew she couldn't blame her ex, Malcolm, or their rocky relationship for the entirety of her despair. But Jesus, it was tempting.

She heard Malcolm's footsteps vibrating on the catwalk outside. She tensed, her eyes darting toward anywhere else. She lifted a clipboard and began to read the list of containers slated to ship out the following day.

The door clattered open and Malcolm huffed as he stepped in. His pervasive scent—a mix of slight body odor and an overused body spray—filled the room. She remembered the brand, could even picture it on his bathroom shelf. She'd felt lust, before, when she'd smelled it. Now it just turned her stomach.

"Evening, Samantha," Malcolm said, leering at her. "Don't suppose you want to hand me my clipboard? Got to check on that container going to Seattle."

"It already left," Sam said, her voice high-pitched and not her own. "And you know better than to call me that."

"I'll keep doing it until it doesn't get a reaction out of you anymore. Fascinating how it still enrages you."

"It doesn't enrage me," Sam insisted. "It just isn't who I am. And you know that."

"Guess I don't know you as well as I thought," Malcolm said, collapsing into his chair and sliding it across the floor. He lifted a girlie magazine from his desk and began to flip through it, perusing the curvaceous women. Sam couldn't help but think his eyes looked like those of dead fish in a market.

"Now, if you don't mind," Sam began retreating to her desk across the room. "I have a lot of paperwork to do, and I know you can't help me with it. Your handwriting is atrocious."

"Ha," Malcolm scoffed. He grabbed the remote control and turned up the volume on the television, and switched it to the news—the only thing that was on after at one in the morning. "Let's see who died in a car accident today, shall we?"

"You're a monster," Sam whispered, not wanting him to hear. Her pulse throbbed to the rhythm of rage. It seemed like a million years ago that her heart soared when he teased her. She'd flip her hair flirtatiously and imagine a future with him. A future? Jesus Christ. She couldn't stand to be in the same room with him now.

The news anchor had shoulder-length blonde hair and was cheery, almost jubilant as she reported on a recent string of carjacking's in the neighboring city. Sam tuned her out. She instead focused on filling out the paperwork required for the next group of containers.

The blonde anchor was cut off suddenly, and a new reporter filled the screen. This man was grim, with a greying face.

"This is breaking news," he announced.

"Ha. It's always 'breaking news,'" Malcolm sneered. "What do you think it is? Some kid's been taken? Someone's been raped again?"

Reluctantly, Sam turned toward the screen, watching the update with mock anticipation.

"We're just getting information of an epidemic, which seems to be affecting people worldwide. Right now, it's unclear as to its precise origin, but we're hearing reports that it's some kind of infection that causes the host to appear rabid or crazed, almost animalistic, then they begin to bite other people. It's believed to be viral in nature, and spreads rapidly. Both private and public facilities are being affected, including grocery stores, movie theaters, shopping districts, and even local government agencies are being overwhelmed. Entire school systems are being shut down until further notice. This is not something to take lightly, as anyone could be affected. Bankers. Secretaries. Lawyers. You need to be cautious."

"Who else?" Malcolm jeered. "Seems like he missed a few people out there. What about shipping yard attendants? What about gravediggers? What about—"

"Just shut up," Sam said. "I'm trying to listen."

"I'm trying to listen," he mocked in a sing-songy voice.

She rolled her eyes and turned up the volume, to block out Malcolm's commentary more than anything else.

"The World Health Organization is strongly advising that you avoid contact with others. That includes family and friends. Right now, it's not clear how many have been infected, but if you begin to show symptoms, isolate yourself, and call the number on your screen. A WHO or CDC representative will assist you."

"Jesus," Sam gasped, standing up so quickly she nearly fell over. "Is this really happening?"

She thought about her sister in Vermont. Had the virus reached the Northeast?

"To recap," the reporter continued, "this virus is extremely contagious, and we all must remain diligent. This is a worldwide epidemic and it goes without saying, all off humanity is at risk. We urge you: until we know more, don't have any contact. With anyone. Period."

"Did he just say don't have contact with anyone on their period?" Malcolm asked, giving her an evil smile.

"Jesus, Malcolm," Sam groaned. "No, he didn't say that."

"He did. I was right here. I heard him." He eased his chair back, eyeing her. "You're not on your period right now, are you?"

"Malcolm," Sam was aghast. "Just shut the hell up."

Malcolm's eyes narrowed. He looked bawdy and rough, like a man with nothing to lose. "Come on, now, Sam."

Sam balked. She saw a glimmer in his eyes that disturbed her. It was proof, once more, that he hadn't stopped lusting after her. Maybe it was even love, if he was capable of it. She doubted it.

"You heard him. He said the world's about to end. You know what that means?"

Sam felt hopeless. "It means we're doomed," she said. "And I'm condemned to stay in this room with you through this whole horrible shift."

"Darling, no. That's not what I meant," Malcolm said, standing from his chair. He stood almost a full foot taller than Sam, and he towered over her now, assessing her. Her blonde locks tumbled over her shoulders, and her blue eyes fluttered like those of a fairytale princess.

She hated that she looked so feminine

sometimes. She chose not to wear makeup during her shifts, not wanting to highlight her appearance.

"Sammy, what I mean is, now that we might be in the last hours of our lives, we shouldn't refrain from touching one another at all. In fact, baby, I think we should strip right now and fuck on the floor, just like we did a year ago. You remember that, Sam? You remember how I made you moan?"

"Stop," Sam said, her voice firm.

"Come on, Sam. You know you want to. Just do it, and we can forget everything that happened."

"Ha. I don't want your forgiveness," she snapped, turning away from him. Her heart still pounded in her chest at the thought of the epidemic. "I don't want anything to do with you. You need to accept that."

"Sam, I can see the way you look at me."

"Like I want to murder you and bury you behind the shipping yard?"

"No. Like you want me to strip you bare and make love to you like a man. You haven't been with a real man in a while. Have you? I know you were dating that little kid—"

"Freddie isn't a kid," Sam said, referring to her neighbor she'd dated briefly. "And he's not my boyfriend."

"So, you saw it, too. That he's just a child," Malcolm grinned.

"No. He was far more mature than you'll ever be," Sam said.

Malcolm lunged and pushed her against the wall. She gasped as he traced the curve of her cheek with a finger. Every cell in her body quivered with fear.

"There, Sammy. Now we've touched. You think I

have the disease? That . . . infection?" Malcolm asked, then snapped his teeth together like a dog.

"I d-don't think I'd know right away," Sam stuttered, trying to stay strong. "And get the fuck off me, or I'll report you."

"Not if it's the end of the world, you won't," he said.

"I wouldn't be with you if you were the last man on Earth." Sam's eyes blazed.

"Oh, baby doll. I think you'll be with me in the end, or you'll regret it." He pressed her harder against the wall. For a single wretched instant, she felt the warmth of his breath on her skin. She was almost certain he'd force his lips on hers.

In a moment of panic, she whipped her head around, just brushing his lips, and looked toward the container yard's security display.

"What the hell?" She ducked under Malcolm's arm and ran toward the video screen. He let her go without a struggle, proving he was all bark, no bite. At least today.

On the display, she saw a convoy of tractor-trailers pulling into the yard, stopping near the observation tower. She couldn't remember seeing a large shipment on the docket.

"We don't have any transports coming in, do we?" she asked.

Malcolm hadn't even bothered to look at the video screen. Having been denied, yet again, he retreated to his girlie magazine and was engrossed once more, his eyes mere inches from the glossy pages. "Not that I recall," he murmured, sounding bored.

"So, you're just going to stop doing your job, now?" she asked.

Malcolm was silent.

She stomped to the radio, lifting the mic and calling down to the yard attendants, who were the real front line at the Universal Container Shipping Company, LLC.

"Hey, Todd," she said, thumbing the button on the radio. "Where's this convoy coming from? I don't have anything on the boards for it."

After a burst of white noise, the reply came through, Todd's southern twang booming from the radio's speaker. "Hey there, Sam. Yep, the trucks were sent over from Helen. But there's no bill of lading."

"Ah. I see," Sam said, her eyebrows furrowing. SOP dictated that without the cargo declared and properly documented, they weren't supposed to allow the containers into the yard. Something tugged at the back of her mind. This had never happened before. But it wasn't like they had anything better to do that night.

"Well, tell you what, Todd. Why don't you open them up and do a quick inventory of the contents. Log everything. You're probably bored down there, anyway, right?"

After a pause, Todd replied, "Yeah, that's about right. Happy to do it."

"Great. Thanks, guys." Sam snapped the mic back into its cradle. She turned toward Malcolm, who was still slouched over, trying to ensure he saw every nook and cranny of the women in his girlie mag.

"I'm going to check things out," she said.

Malcolm snorted. He gave no indication of joining her. Sam burst out the side door, to the catwalk surrounding their office. The air was oddly chilly. But with the news from the television still ringing in her ears, she felt eerily alive.

At the edge of the catwalk, she looked out over the shipping yard below, her arms wide and her hands gripping the railing. She watched as Todd, a nearly seven-foot tall, broad-shouldered man, spoke to several of the workers he supervised, explaining the orders. Sam began to chew manically at the dead skin on her lip.

Malcolm appeared beside her. He kept his distance, no longer spewing ugliness. He, too, gripped the railing. Like it or not, they were still co-workers, no matter what drama still sizzled between them.

Todd lifted a lever at the rear of the first trailer, cracking the container open. He craned his neck, peering into the darkness. A look of horror painted his face. His eyes widened, gleaming stark white. Several screaming humans leaped from the depths of the container, wrapping their limbs around him. One of them, a woman, put her mouth on Todd's throat and tore at his skin, bringing a large waterfall of blood pouring from his neck. He had no time to scream—the woman dug her teeth deeper, taking out his vocal cords.

"What the fuck?" Sam cried, gripping the rail tightly. The sight of Todd's blood caused her stomach to clench, and for a split second, she thought was going to be sick. Dozens more of the crazed people erupted from the container, one or two going to the next container and freeing more of them.

"They're working as a pack," Sam muttered, both horrified and fascinated. "They know exactly what they're doing." Shock distanced her from the sight. She felt above it all, as if she were a god, looking down at her disciples.

The other men in the shipping yard had already been attacked or were sprinting away, their limbs thrashing, their panic too all-encompassing for them to scream.

"Fuckin' a, man!" Malcolm howled, sounding almost overjoyed. Sam gaped at him, horrified at the amusement on his face. He flailed his arms wildly. "Look, baby. This is exactly what I mean. You had your chance back there with me. You had your chance to fuck me before you die. And now, everything's about to get real." He laughed manically. "I bet you didn't know the world would end when you dumped me. Bet you thought you had a big, wild, beautiful life in front of you. Guess you never know, huh?"

Sam didn't respond. She took a step back, wanting distance herself from him. Far below, she heard one of the crazed monsters leap upon another member of the shipping yard crew, clawing at him. He cried out her name. "SAM!" She didn't want to know who it was. She didn't want to see his face before he died.

"Malcolm," Sam said finally, swallowing her terror. Inwardly, she was trying to focus, trying to avoid an impending panic attack. Her eyes filled with tears. "Malcolm, we have to call this in. We have to tell someone what's going on."

But Malcolm just laughed again. Louder, bouncier, more cartoony. Sam covered her ears, trying to will this reality away.

"Darling, you saw the news. You knew this was coming. You just didn't think it would happen so soon. It's just like you to think you'll be safe, in your own little bubble," Malcolm said, practically spitting with glee. "Our best bet, *darling*, is to get the fuck away from here. As far as we can."

Sam pushed past him heading toward the office. She stepped inside, reached for the phone and began to dial her sister's number, needing to hear a rational voice, a voice of reason. She needed to talk to someone who wasn't an imbecile. But as she dialed the phone, the power clipped off inside the observation tower, and the phone went dead in her hand. She couldn't see a thing—not even the paneled wall mere inches from of her face. She began to shiver violently, sensing Malcolm behind her. She could still smell his horrendous body odor. Outside, she heard a scream that seemed to ricochet off the containers and the warehouse wall, back and forth, until it faded away.

"We're going to die here, aren't we?" she whispered, her own voice sounding foreign to her.

But Malcolm didn't reply. Instead, he leaned close to her and started breathing heavily on her neck, as if he, like the crazed monsters outside, wanted to eat her whole.

2.

R alph's screams echoed through the dank air of the surrounding woodland. Clay grabbed the ragged older man's shoulders, shoving him against a nearby tree. The man's face was panicked, and his mismatched arms dangled uselessly, making him look like a rag doll.

"I'm so sorry, Clay," Ralph wept hysterically. "If I just had my right hand—"

Clay tried to reassure his friend, but he had to stay calm himself. A few feet away, Leland Jacobs was tying a rag over a gunshot wound on Brandon's upper arm. Brandon was sweating profusely, beads of it coursing down his forehead and cheeks. His eyes caught Clay's, communicating silently, before turning his attention back to the blood-soaked rag.

"I thought they had me surrounded," Ralph said, his words calmer now. "I wasn't ready, Clay. I just started shooting. Jesus. And Brandon—he, he just came out of nowhere—"

"You just haven't practiced enough with your left hand, yet," Clay said quietly. "Let's give it a rest for now."

"I can't—" Ralph said, sounding like a child. "I just can't do this anymore, Clay." Snot began to run from his nostrils.

Clay looked around, searching for the rest of their party. God, every step seemed to bring another disaster. The crazed monsters they'd killed in the recent attack lay in thick pools of their own blood, adding that all too familiar, dead skunk stench to the air. Clay had learned to breathe through it. He supposed they all had.

"You holding up over there, Brandon?" Clay asked, still holding Ralph.

Brandon nodded meekly. He'd turned eighteen in the weeks since they'd left Carterville, mentioning his birthday gruffly to Clay as they'd walked along the outskirts of the city. Clay had clapped him on the back, wishing he had some kind of advice for him. After all, he was an adult now. He should have had his entire life in front of him. But as it was, he might only have a week. A day, or even just an hour. And now he was shot, his blood soaking through the bandage.

"See. He's going to be fine," Clay said, pushing down his churning emotions. He eyed Ralph's right arm, the wrist ending in a stump, wrapped in bandages they'd been able to salvage from the wreck. "Don't wear yourself out worrying, man. You need to rest up."

Ralph spat on the ground before dropping to his knees, and raised his head to the sky. It looked like he was praying, but Clay knew better. He leaned back on the ground, listening to Jacobs as he bound Brandon's upper arm.

The struggle had really started the moment they'd headed out of Carterville. Clay had watched the energy field flicker off and on for over an hour before attempting to pass, hoping he'd caught the pattern. They'd loaded themselves up, strapped on their seat belts and crossed themselves for good measure. But as they'd lurched through the energy field, the alien green flash arced over them, rolling the fully loaded Humvee onto its side.

The back of the vehicle, which had taken the brunt of the green force field, immediately burst into flames. They'd all unstrapped themselves quickly—everyone except Ralph. He screamed in a ragged, deep-throated voice. Brandon and Daniels had tossed supplies from the back of the burning vehicle, trying to grab the most important things, like bullets. Ralph, in the meantime, had continued wailing, his arm pinned.

"CLAY! I'M STUCK!" he'd cried, sounding demented with terror. "GET ME THE HELL OUT OF HERE!"

Clay had leaped back into the now-blistering vehicle, finding that Ralph's arm was trapped between the seat and the damaged metal frame. Clay began to yank at Ralph's arm, trying to free him. But the skin just tore, and blood came spewing from his veins.

"I can feel the flames, Clay!" Ralph cried. The fire began to lick at their ears, singeing the back of Ralph's long, hillbilly hair. "Jesus. I'm going to join Connie, now, aren't I? Connie!" He began to weep, looking resigned, tears dropping on his shirt.

Clay had hesitated for only an instant before he pulled a large knife from his back pocket and begun to hack at Ralph's forearm as the fire inched nearer. Ralph looked shocked, aghast, the color draining from his face. When the bone separated, Ralph spewed an ocean of green vomit that resembled the blood of the crazed monsters. In a moment of panic, he yanked at his arm a final time—it was already free. He blinked wildly at it, seeing the stump for the first time. Clay wound Ralph's collar around his hand and dragged him out of the thick, black smoke.

They had fallen back on the ground, coughing spasmodically. Ralph had nearly blacked out when Jacobs started to tend to his bleeding arm, cursing them for not saving the first aid supplies from the fire. No one had replied, listening instead to the weak, muffled cries of their wounded friend.

Since then, they'd been walking, meandering toward Helen. The trip was about six hours by vehicle. But with the injuries, their fatigue, and being on foot, it was much longer, wearing them thin.

The worst part was that they had to fight off the deranged, used-to-be people at every turn. The crazed had begun to learn, sneaking up behind them, preying on the stragglers of the group. They'd leap on their backs, wrapping their arms around their necks and squealing. When this happened, another member of their group—normally Daniels—stopped the crazed with a bullet to the brain.

They had to be alert constantly.

And now, one of their own had put a bullet through Brandon. Just eighteen years old, and forever scarred.

"I'm just not used to this," Ralph wept on. Brandon lost consciousness nearby.

"None of us are," Clay agreed, pulling Ralph up from the ground, seeing a convenience store nearby. "Let's get under cover. We can't very well stay out here, waiting for the next attack."

He lifted Ralph, carrying his frail frame easily. Brandon returned briefly to consciousness, and allowed Jacobs to help him to his feet. The four of them eased toward the convenience store as clouds began to fill the sky. Clay didn't know what time it was, or even the day. Thursday? Monday? It didn't matter anymore.

3.

I nside the convenience store, Ralph went around the counter, shuffling toward the cash register. As if money could help them during the apocalypse, Clay thought bitterly.

Brandon slid into a lawn chair, cradling his arm. Jacobs eyed Clay and gestured away from the others, wanting to speak with him privately. His eyes reflected a truth that Clay surely didn't want to hear.

"Is he going to be all right?" Clay asked, as they stood in the looted snack aisle, amid empty chip bags.

"It's just a flesh wound. This time," Jacobs said quietly.

"Oh, thank god," Clay sighed. "What do you mean, this time?"

"I mean, I'm not the right person to be dealing with shit like this," Jacobs said, his eyes dark. "I'm a scientist. I'm not a real doctor. I had maybe three classes on human anatomy, over ten years ago. Next time something like this happens—and it's a gut wound, instead of an arm wound—we won't be so lucky."

Clay felt his fury building. "We all have to do the best we can, Leland," he said. "And doing what you can for us, with your limited knowledge, means exactly that. Do you understand?"

Jacobs didn't reply. As they faced off, they could hear Ralph's guilt-ridden whimpers and Brandon's soft moans of pain.

"Brandon. Hey, kid," Ralph said, finally taking notice of someone else's suffering. He eased toward the boy, his eyes rodent-like in the dim light. He still wasn't able to look at his victim. "Hey. I'm so, so sorry, Brandon."

Clay and Jacobs watched silently. Clay sensed that tension could build between them, the kind that threatened the delicate balance in their small band of survivors. He closed his eyes tightly, willing some kind of forgiveness.

"Seriously. I just ain't got used to this bum arm yet," Ralph said.

"Neither have I," Brandon replied quietly.

Ralph and Brandon stared at each other for a long time, animosity growing. Clay had half a mind to speak up, to find words that sounded appropriately leader-like, that would unite his tribe again. But as he went to step forward, Ralph stretched out his arm, stopping him.

"No, sheriff. Don't sweet talk him. He can feel however he wants."

"I forgive you," Brandon said, after slight hesitation. "I do. I know it was an accident. And I think it'll heal. Okay? You happy?"

Ralph closed his eyes, as if he was receiving absolution from a priest. He dropped to his bony knees, looking again like he was mid-prayer.

Clay started to speak, to suggest that they talk about their next move, to not waste time in the silence.

But he didn't have time.

Alayna and Daniels burst into the convenience store, their guns pointed at the ceiling, spattered with dirt and gore. Alayna caught Clay's eye before reporting.

"They're all dead out there. Daniels and I chased them out about a mile, killed them all. Should be clear for a bit if we want to rest."

"Wonderful news," Clay said with relief. He smiled at Alayna warmly, but she didn't return it.

Her eyes darted toward Daniels, who added, "But the bad news is, we only have about fifty or so rounds of ammunition left." Reminding them, once more, of how close they were to death.

"Jesus Christ," Brandon said, wrapping his hand gingerly around his bandages. "We're fucked."

No one spoke.

Daniels slung his rifle in one swift motion.

"But there were cars in the distance," Alayna added. "A big cluster of them. Maybe three miles up. We could see them across the field."

"Any sign of the crazed up there?" Clay asked.

"We couldn't see any. At least, not from where we were," Alayna said.

"Oh, and I suppose you two want to run up there and see what all the fuss is about?" Ralph said sarcastically. "That's all this has been, hasn't it? Just one curiosity after another. And meanwhile, I've lost half an arm. And Brandon's been shot."

Clay didn't remind Ralph that he was the perpetrator. He sighed, scanning the convenience store. It was cozy, still decently stocked with various canned goods, and featured a long row of lawn chairs along one wall. They would be comfortable there, at least for a while. But Jesus Christ, Clay thought, growing anxious. He had to get to Helen to try to find his wife and daughter. He glanced at Alayna, whom he'd lusted after just days before. He could sense a need in her, as well. For Megan.

"You want to stay?" Clay asked. "Then, stay. You don't have to listen to me anymore, if you want to be on your own. But Alayna and I have to move on. We have to get to our people. And I'm not stopping here for days to rest. We'll just die here a little bit slower than we'd die out there."

Jacobs said, "I need to find the rest of my team, as well. The other scientists who know about the nanites. It's absolutely imperative."

Clay nodded, and glared at Ralph. "You see there? It's imperative. I'm sure that's not a word you use often, so let's break it down for you—"

"Shhh—" Alayna cut him off. "Don't make it worse."

Ralph and Brandon eyed each other. Silence settled over them, reflecting the indecision. Brandon tried to sit up. "What do you think, Big Ralph?" he asked, trying a nickname on the man for the first time. "You think we should keep going, or stick around?"

Ralph hesitated, unaccustomed to making decisions. He scratched at his tearstained cheek and his eyes flickered toward Clay, assessing him. "If we stay, Brandon, that means we'll be on our own. No more ammunition. No more—well . . . no more help."

"That's true. But fuck it. I'm already shot." Brandon's voice was challenging, almost asking Ralph to take on the horrible prospect. "What's a few weeks of staying, eating as much food as we possibly can, and then getting eaten up by those crazed monsters, huh? Doesn't sound all that bad to me."

Ralph shrunk into himself, looking fearful. He

swiped his only hand over his scalp, almost certainly thinking about Connie's touch. He'd looked like less of a person since she'd died.

"You all have someone," he spat. "Clay, you've got Alayna. And Jacobs and Daniels. Hell, Brandon, you and Alayna care about each other. You're close as can be. But me? None of you would care if I lived or died. You should have left me in that burning Humvee, you bastard," he said, zeroing in on Clay. "I don't want to live anymore. I don't want to be—"

Brandon interrupted him, staggering up from his chair, still holding his arm. "Ralph, that's not true. I've looked up to you since this started. I'd hate it if you died. You seem to forget that I lost a sister at the beginning of all of this."

Ralph was wide-eyed, like a deer seeing a hunter. He gulped and stood a bit straighter. "Wh—what?" he stuttered. "Brandon, do you really mean it? That you'd miss me?"

"Of course I mean it, you old bastard," Brandon said. "Just don't fucking shoot me again. Okay?"

"Deal," Ralph whispered, offering his hand to Brandon. Their eyes met for a moment, friendship making them equals, regardless of their difference in age.

Despite everything, Clay's heart softened at the camaraderie, giving him a brief interlude from the horror that was now their life. Again, he tried to catch Alayna's eye, but her face had turned pale green, and she'd started to tremble—something she'd been doing recently—that chilled Clay to the bone. But he couldn't find the courage to ask her about it, not after their night together.

Ralph was wrong, Clay realized then. He didn't have Alayna. Not anymore. He was currently living with the ghosts in his head: his wife and his daughter, in the hope they'd be back in his life soon. But he couldn't afford to be optimistic. None of them could. It was the end of the world, after all.

4.

"We'll stockpile as much food as we can," Clay announced a few minutes later as the tension in the room eased. Brandon and Ralph now sat companionably side by side, one of Ralph's knees crossed casually over the other, as if it was just an ordinary day.

"I think all the good food's spoiled," Alayna said, nodding at the coolers. "And we won't survive long on junk food."

"Honey, it's the apocalypse," Daniels retorted. "We'll have to survive on whatever preservative-filled thing the government tried to kill us with. It's all we have now."

"We'll get weaker with every bite," Alayna said, frowning. "Candy bars? Chips? Clay, you've got to be kidding me."

"Suggest a better option, then," Clay said, his hand on his holster.

Alayna was silent. The rest of the crew was already resigned to their potato chip lifestyle. Clay's stomach ached, just at the thought. But they were hungry, desperately so. And they hadn't seen any wildlife to hunt. What happened to all the deer? To the dogs, even? Had they been eaten up by the monsters, becoming as source of fuel?

Clay drifted toward the back of the store, with Jacobs following. Near the toiletries, he found a large selection of sacks and duffel bags, enough for them to carry the food with, if they strapped them to their backs like camels. He scooped up as many as he could carry, and dropped them in front of the others.

"Get as much as you can. I think I saw some beef jerky near the register. That might be our best bet for protein." He eyed Alayna again. Why did she seem to glare at him with such scornful eyes?

Ralph lifted a sack tentatively.

"And dump all the soda bottles," Clay told them. "We'll fill the soda bottles with fresh water from the tap."

"Ah, shit," Brandon said, easing one of the twist tops from a bottle. "I used to drink tons of this stuff every single day, with money I got from my after school job. And now it's right here. For free."

"That shit will kill you," Alayna insisted.

"If this is the thing that kills me when there are monsters on the loose, then I choose this," Brandon said, chugging Mountain Dew. He wiped his hand over his mouth, blinking wildly. "It really burns when you're not used to it."

"That's because it's not natural," Alayna said, her eyebrows high. "Your body doesn't really digest it."

"Just a few more sips," Brandon murmured, drinking as much as he could of the yellow liquid.

Ralph patted his shoulder, chuckling. "He's a boy after my own heart. We love the things that will destroy us. Hell, I'd be smoking more of these free cigarettes if I knew they wouldn't slow me down. I'd be so out of breath all the time, I probably wouldn't be able to keep up with you all. So, Kid? You want to try a cigarette?"

"As if I haven't smoked before," Brandon scoffed. It was obvious to all of them that he hadn't, that he was covering up his "embarrassing" teenage existence, which was probably far cleaner than he admitted.

"All right, then," Ralph said, reaching for the Marlboro Reds. He fumbled with the plastic and then opened it, revealing the triple rows of tan-tipped cigarettes. He took two, handed one to Brandon and snagged a lighter from near the cash register.

"Don't smoke in here," Alayna insisted. "The rest of us have to live with it."

"I think I'd like one of those." Daniels reached a large, calloused hand toward the box. "Hell, it might be the last one I ever smoke."

"Guys. Stop it," Clay snapped. His mind was racing with thoughts of his daughter and wife, and of all the time they were wasting. He saw red for an instant. Was this panic? "We have to fill our bags and get moving."

He stomped toward the back of the store, hearing Ralph and Daniels flick their lighters. The smell of smoke reached him a few moments later.

"You going to try it, Brandon?" Ralph asked.

"I told you. I already have," Brandon said.

"You don't want another one?" Ralph asked, clearly amused.

"I think I'll stick to my Mountain Dew, if that's okay."

"Suit yourself."

Brandon joined Clay in the hunt for food supplies, grabbing cans of beans and other vegetables and filling his sacks. Alayna busied herself near the corner, sliding her fingers over the once-familiar boxes of macaroni and cheese and rice—things that weren't practical, given that they were always on the move, and it was far too dangerous to start a fire.

Clay worked his way closer to Alayna, wanting to understand why their relationship had soured. They'd made passionate love not so long ago, and now they looked at each other like total strangers.

"I remember you used to eat this macaroni and cheese crap almost every day for lunch," Alayna said as he drew closer to her, her voice a whisper. "Your wife would pack you delicious lunches, with protein to make you healthier. But you'd always head to the store and buy this." She gave him a teasing smile, her eyes twinkling.

Finally, Clay thought. They could bond over their memories.

"I was addicted to it. I think we can blame it, single-handedly, for all my weight gain," he laughed. "Too bad we can't serve some up now."

Alayna tilted her bag toward him, showing her collection. "Peanuts. Almonds. Cashews. I think that'll stick to our bones, at least for a while."

Clay nodded, meeting her eyes for a moment. He wanted to say something, to apologize for any tension between them, to prove that he wanted to remain friends—the closest of friends, especially as everything grew more dire. But he couldn't speak.

"Sorry it isn't getting any easier," he said instead. "I know you want to see Megan."

Alayna slid her fingers through her coarse hair. "I just want to make sure she's all right. I don't know what that means for us, you know. She did sleep with Daniels." Her eyes narrowed slightly. "I don't think I'm even that upset. There are no real rules out here, are there?"

"I'm not sure I can answer that truthfully," Clay said wryly. They were at the bottom of the world, looking up. It seemed impossible that they could ever clamber back up to where they belonged.

They continued to pack, Brandon stuffing in a massive collection of candy and granola bars, much to the chagrin of Alayna. She rolled her eyes and ran her hand over his hair, acting almost motherly. Clay was reminded of Valerie—how she'd roll her eyes at their daughter Maia's silly quirks, and her insistence that "just one more snack" wouldn't hurt. God, he'd had such a beautiful family. But now, this rag-tag troop of stragglers, trying to stay alive—this was his family.

"We all set?" Clay asked, strapping several sacks to his back and grabbing his gun, looking at each of them in turn for confirmation.

They gathered in a line facing the once-automatic doors of the convenience store. The light outside shimmered on the glass. For a moment, Clay felt almost at peace, stocked with food supplies, strong in the companionship of these people.

Then, Ralph broke his reverie. "Shit! You see them, Clay? There, by the gas pumps? They see us too, I reckon."

Clay moved up and peered out the window. Sure enough, a small horde of the crazed were wavering toward them, their rotting arms waving and dripping blood.

"All right, gang. Let's do what we've been training to do." Clay squared his shoulders. "We don't have time to mess around."

5.

C lay turned toward Brandon and Ralph. The pair nodded curtly, with Daniels behind them, racking a bullet into the chamber of his rifle. No one spoke for several seconds as the crazed monsters poured across the road, leaving bloody tracks on the pavement. One of them was wailing, a guttural, inhuman sound, reminiscent of a dying cow.

"Aim well, gang," Clay said, turning his eyes back to the door. "And try use only one bullet per zombie. We can't afford any more than that. And we definitely can't afford any more disasters, a la Ralph and Brandon. Is that clear?"

Clay led the team out onto the pavement. The first onslaught of the crazed was just six or seven that Clay and Daniels took with quick, accurate shots. The monsters didn't even make it to the sidewalk.

But the chaos attracted still more of the crazed. The survivors began to spread out, each holding their own, dropping the monsters. Clay glanced up when Alayna yelped at a bony hand on her back. She spun, putting a bullet between the crazed's teeth, and then another between his eyes. His blood spattered her before he fell. Without hesitation, she returned to the fray, killing two more monsters in rapid succession.

Clay felt a moment of sincere pride before he, too, was forced to focus on the onslaught.

It was all becoming normal, almost second nature. Murder. Constant, every day murder. It was their way of life.

Brandon and Ralph were next to each other and blasting through the crazed like cowboys. Brandon spewed curse words with a hoarse, teenage voice as he fired, clearly mimicking actions from a fantasy or video game. Ralph was concentrating fiercely, less accurate for having to use his left hand.

Jacobs and Daniels fought with similar styles, despite Daniels' obvious years of training and Jacobs' rather weak technique. They plugged each of the crazed monsters at least twice to be sure. They were ignoring Clay's plea to conserve ammunition. But Jacobs was too terrified to handle it any other way. And Daniels was too aggressive, wanting to retaliate with as much force as he could.

After a small eternity with the swarming crazed, Clay realized there were only a few more to put down. Off to the side, Ralph backed away from his position, suddenly looking fearful. He dropped to his knees, crying out. Clay couldn't make out the words.

Brandon jumped next to him. He blasted two that were approaching rapidly, becoming Ralph's guardian. Brandon killed the last three, dropping them to the blood-soaked pavement, their limbs still flailing helplessly.

Brandon breathed hard in the silence that followed, and squinted down at his friend. Ralph's eyes were tightly closed, panic still on his face.

"What was that, man?" Brandon asked. He gripped Ralph's elbow and pulled him to his feet. "Jesus. You're better than that."

"I'm not," Ralph whimpered. "I'm just not." He dropped to his knees and cowered, trying to cover his ears. "That fucking gunfire is destroying my eardrums, Brandon. I can't take it anymore. I'm going fucking nuts. This—this is why they put the soldiers in the loony bins, Brandon. It's because of the gunfire."

Clay and the others joined Brandon and Ralph, but gave them several feet of space. Ralph was panting, as if he couldn't take in enough air. Brandon finally kneeled down beside him and murmured into his ear, as if he were consoling a child.

"Ralph, you can't give up on me like that. Not out here, not on the battlefield. We only have each other now. And I told you back in the store that I'd be really bummed if you died. Listen, man. I meant it. I wouldn't get over it, Ralph. Think about me when you're out here. Think about Alayna. Think about how Connie would want you to live, for Christ's sake."

Clay's eyes narrowed, meeting Alayna's. She pressed her lips together, a look of concern on her face. Ralph was on the brink of insanity. It seemed clear to both of them.

"Plus, I know you're not going to shoot me again," Brandon said, trying to joke. "Because you know I'll shoot you back if you do."

"Ha," Ralph said. A single tear tracked through the dirt on his cheek. "It's not that, kid. I just ran out of bullets in the gun, you know? And I didn't have another hand to reload. I'm useless. I'm completely useless to you guys out here. I was ready to surrender. Give up. I'm just holding y'all back, anyway."

"That's not true," Brandon said, rubbing at the

old man's back. "We're going to get out of this. We're going to survive. Giving up is never an option. And if you need someone to change out your clips, I got you next time. Friends watch out for each other."

Ralph peered at the rapidly maturing young man suspiciously. "Why should an old man like me trust a kid like you?"

"I already saved your life once, asshole," Brandon replied. "Don't forget that for a minute. You owe me. And the only thing I want is for you to live, dammit. Live!"

Everyone moved closer to the man and boy, galvanized by Brandon's speech. His strength and compassion made them stand straighter, and their eyes brighter. They'd had to throw out all the rules of their past lives. Age was just a number, now. Nothing more.

Brandon helped Ralph up. Both were spattered with blood from the crazed. Clay knew he should say something, find words that would bring them together. But exhaustion from the day numbed him.

"We have to keep moving," he said finally. "We can't waste the whole day."

They nodded before silently collecting their sacks of food. Brandon popped open a can of Pringles and began to chomp, a smile stretching his cheeks. Clay had half a mind to tell him that he'd done a good thing, and that he'd be a good leader one day. Maybe even a sheriff, if he wanted it.

But he kept it to himself, the future was too uncertain. He kept his eyes on the horizon, his mind worried about the difficult road ahead.

6.

They walked through the afternoon, their shoes tighter on their feet with every mile. Their muscles were achy, their eyes were glazed. Clay forced himself on, despite the vertigo creeping in. Daniels, who was a bit taller, walked amicably beside him, his boots crunching on the occasional pebble.

"You think we'll have to walk all the way there?" Daniels asked, trying to make his question private. But his voice was far louder than intended. The others perked up, listening.

"I've been trying to come up with something . . . anything that could protect us from this heat and get us under some kind of cover," Clay said, still watching the road in front of them. "But so far, nothing. I'm thinking maybe we should find shelter for the night soon. There's not much daylight left, and I don't want to be out here after dark."

The terrain around them had changed in the previous hour, the road now skirting the rim of a massive canyon on one side, snaking through the bordering mountains. As they followed the curvature of the road, Clay stopped short, hopeful at what just came into view.

In front of them were six cars, stopped haphazardly on the road. In the distance, an oversized semi truck had jackknifed, blocking the road. The fifth wheel coupling and forward half of the trailer jutted beyond the edge of the canyon, threatening to go over at any moment.

"Jesus," Clay murmured, trying to make sense of the scene.

"What are we waiting for?" Daniels cried. "We should try to get one of the cars started. It might be cramped, but at least we'd have some shelter on the way to Helen."

"And how do we drive it around that semi?" Alayna asked, her nose high. "There's no median to drive on. We'd just drive straight into the canyon."

"And explode into a million pieces," Ralph added.

"Right," Alayna agreed. "It's a complete bottleneck."

"Well, damn." Daniels scratched at his growing beard.

"Then we check all the cars, and scavenge anything useful," Clay said. "We'll keep going on foot, but we might find more supplies at least."

"I'm sure everyone took anything of value with them," Jacobs pointed out.

"Well, it doesn't hurt to look," Clay said, his eyes alert. "Alayna. Adam. You stand guard. We're losing light quickly. Make sure the crazed don't come at us. And let out a yell if you see something, anything. You're our eyes and ears."

"Got it," Alayna said.

The rest of them hurried forward, circling the first vehicle, a dark green sedan. It sat at an angle, the right rear tire hanging over the edge. Clay peered into it, pressing his forehead against the glass, and saw nothing but black leather seats and a few empty soda bottles in back. He tried the door and it opened.

He leaned toward the glove box, finding nothing but insurance papers for a man named Matthew Connors, and a toy. He sighed, looking up at Ralph, Brandon, and Jacobs, standing nearby with blank looks on their faces.

"I'll check the trunk and the back seat. Why don't you three start on the other vehicles. We should look through everything. Leave no seat unturned. Understand?"

They headed toward the other cars; beginning their own methodical searches. They dove through abandoned personal items, discovering what was left behind by people who were either now dead or at least long gone. Alayna and Daniels paced the perimeter, their guns high, their eyes sharp. The sun was dipping lower, adding to Clay's mounting anxiety.

Several minutes later, Clay joined the other three. Brandon was squeezed in the backseat of a car, rifling through a briefcase. "Nothing but papers, man. I found some snacks up front, though. Fruit roll-ups. I used to love that shit."

Disheartened, Clay raised his eyebrows at Jacobs across the top of the car. Jacobs shrugged and moved on to the next vehicle. But as he neared the red SUV, he stopped, his shoulders tensing. He was frozen, panicked.

"Jacobs? Leland? What is it?" Clay asked.

"I—I think you're going to want to see this," Jacobs said quietly. "Brandon. Stay back."

"Why? You can't leave me out of the loop," Brandon said indignantly.

Clay joined Jacobs at the SUV. Even with the glare from the sun, he could see the interior clearly. The scene made his blood run cold. This was the reality they were all now facing; this was death and destruction. This was the future of their world.

A middle-aged man sat in the driver's seat, a bullet wound at the side of his head. Dried blood on his cheek and down his shirt. His mouth was agape, and his eyes were half-open and oddly purple. Beside him, a younger woman, looking peaceful but with a similar bullet wound just north of her ear. In the back seat, two children, both pre-teens, huddled together, covered in blood.

"Jesus Christ," Clay gasped.

"What do you want to do, boss?" Jacobs murmured, making no effort to reach for the door handle. "I don't know if we should disturb them. Who knows how long they've been in there."

Brandon and Ralph appeared beside them. Brandon gasped and smacked his hand over his mouth. Ralph was stoic, unshakable now. They both looked away, clearly wishing they were somewhere else.

"All—um, all the other cars are cleared," Brandon said, drifting away from the gruesome scene. "Where would their passengers have gone?"

Clay eyed the gorge beside them with curiosity, wondering what they might find. He shivered, suspecting that all of the cars' drivers were either plastered to the canyon floor and dead, or munched up at the hands of the crazed. Perhaps they were crazed themselves.

"You think the dad took matters into his own hands, then?" Ralph asked. "Something made him crack. And he knew he had to be the one to kill his family. He brought them into the world. He'll take them out of it. That sort of thing?"

Clay nodded almost imperceptibly. He thought

about Maia and Valerie. Faced with the same choice, would he have shot them? He imagined aiming the gun at each of their heads. Forcing himself to squeeze the trigger. He shivered.

"I would never be able to kill Connie," Ralph whispered as if Connie wasn't already dead. "It would destroy me."

"He didn't have to live with his decision long." Brandon gestured at the sad, lifeless man in the front seat. "He's gone."

"This means he has a gun," Clay realized with a start.

"We should just leave them in peace, Clay—" Ralph began tentatively. "I don't want to open it."

"We have to think about survival," Clay said, sounding brutish. He brought the top of his shirt over his nose and mouth, hoping to block the smell. He yanked at the door and opened their coffin. Putrid air poured out. Up close, he could see horrible details about the children: that the girl had ribbons woven into her hair, bright blue. That the older brother still had long-since-silent ear buds stuffed in his ears.

The father's face was easier to bear. The man was fatigued, clearly. Probably frazzled to no end during his final days of life, strapping his family into their SUV and trying to hightail it out of town. Clay reached in and grabbed the gun from the man's hand, then dug through the side compartment and found several more rounds. Clay felt a momentary burst of hope.

"We got some," he said, still studying the vehicle with morbid curiosity.

"Shit, man," Jacobs murmured as Clay closed the door. "I'm glad it was you who went in there, not me."

Clay put the gun in his waistband and pocketed the bullets, blowing hard several times attempting to clear the stench from his nose. The silence around him was dense and thick, imbued with despair. Would they soon be as dead as these innocent people? Should they just shoot one another now and avoid all this?

Were they just as doomed?

Clay shook his head and moved on to the semi. The others followed.

When he popped open the cab door, the first thing he checked was the CB, tapping the button but hearing no static on the other end. The seat was set back, showing the driver had been a long-legged person. A green tree air freshener danced from the edge of the visor above, and a photograph of a young girl, with the words: "HI DADDY" was taped to the dashboard. Clay was grateful he didn't have to look at another body.

"No power, I guess," Clay said and returned to the ground. "And no sign of extra supplies up there, either. Unless you want a cassette of Journey's greatest hits."

"Hey. They have some good ones," Ralph protested. "At least we know our absent driver had good taste in music."

"My guess is he came on some of the crazed in the road," Jacobs said. "Swerved trying to avoid them. The tires locked up—"

Brandon shook his head. "I don't really want to think about what happened."

Alayna appeared, with Daniels following close behind. She pointed her thumb at the back of the trailer, shrugging. "We tried to open it up, but it's locked. Any sign of the key up there?"

"The key?" Clay was almost giddy. He bounded to the back, drew his gun confidently and blew the lock off. It skittered off the edge and into the canyon, becoming just a small dot before completely disappearing from view.

Clay opened the trailer and gaped at the load. He whooped with triumph. When the others saw inside, they added their voices to his. They'd finally caught a break. Of course, their luck could run out any moment.

"Shit." Ralph spat on the ground. "I never thought I'd say this, especially not now. But it seems our prayers have been answered, guys." He smacked Brandon on the back, and he squealed in mock pain.

The others laughed and cheered, raising their arms as if they'd just won a race. They had nothing but the road anymore. And now they would make the road their bitch.

7.

A high-pitched whine echoed through the canyon, bouncing around the red rock formations, and making the bright, orange sunset come to life in a way that seemed impossible, given the post-apocalyptic nature of the previous few weeks.

Clay had never felt more alive.

The survivors tore down the road, riding six mopeds, leaning into the wind. The mopeds had been in the back of the trailer, apparently on their way to a local dealership. There'd been twelve of them in all—more than enough.

"Have you guys ever ridden one of these?" Brandon had asked, giving them a dose of his teenage arrogance. "Because I have. And they're rad."

"I think we all know how to ride, thanks," Alayna retorted.

"It's different." Brandon smiled. "You feel more alive. Just trust me on this one."

But once they'd pushed their mopeds around the bottleneck and barreled toward Helen, Clay had to admit, he understood Brandon's feelings. The wind tugged at his hair, made his cheeks red, and chapped his lips. But he screamed out a cowboy-ish yell, with the blood pumping in his veins.

Brandon was next to him in the left-hand lane, dangerously close to the edge of the canyon. But his eyes were wide and full of laughter—he was quite aware how reckless his actions were—and he wouldn't have changed them for the world.

Alayna passed Clay and pulled ahead, giving him a sassy look, her eyes dancing. She sped forward, taking the lead, while Clay laughed heartily.

Clay spotted a sign that read, Helen—30. That would take them no time at all, they'd probably arrive before dark.

They were going to make it. They were one step closer to finding where Valerie and Maia were—hopefully learning Megan's whereabouts, as well—and getting a step closer to normality, something that had become more dream-like and distant with every passing hour.

When they exited from the highway into the outskirts of town, Clay slowed and turned his head toward Jacobs. "Pull over!" he yelled, then slowed his bike to a stop and cut his engine. The others joined him, and they all looked over the high road at the city in the valley. Clay thought it was the most beautiful sight he'd seen in a while: so far away from depths of the destruction of civilization.

"Where exactly are we going, anyway?" Ralph asked.

Clay searched the others' faces, landing finally on Jacobs. His lips were pressed firmly together; his eyes were hard, knowledgeable.

"I don't know my way around Helen," Clay said. "Only a vague recollection of where Main Street is," he prodded Jacobs for answers.

"The candy shop," Jacobs said pointing at the town. "It's on Main Street, in fact."

"When were you here last?" Clay asked.

"Just a few weeks ago. We were archiving files in the lab downstairs. But I have reason to believe the other scientists stayed behind. Like I wanted to, back at our lab."

"You're saying that was the reasonable option?" Alayna said incredulously. "We would have died back there."

"We still don't know what we're going to find down there," Clay said. "Let's not bicker. Let's just get in there. See what we can see. If they're there, great. If they've moved on, then so will we."

In reality, he didn't want to get his hopes up. But just the thought of seeing some different faces, getting some new information, after so much doubt and nothingness, revved Clay's soul. And if Jacobs' scientists were around, he knew that they'd be that much closer to understanding the epidemic, and understanding if they could live through it.

"You lead, Jacobs," Clay said. "If we see any of the crazed, or any survivors for that matter, don't stop. It's too dangerous, and it's getting dark. We need to get to the lab. Does everyone understand?"

Jacobs revved his engine and pulled out first, leaving Clay to follow. The rest rode single-file behind him. They drove tentatively into Helen, feeling the chill as the day waned. The next hour could change their survival tactics, and thus, the rest of their lives.

8.

Despite being twice the size in population, Helen was similar to Carterville in almost every way, with the same string of gas stations and fast food joints littering the main drag. Post-epidemic, the town was virtually deserted, much like Carterville, with dusk drawing long shadows across the pavement.

Seeing Helen so desolate sent shivers down Clay's spine. He kept his eyes on the horizon, ensuring that his crew wasn't riding headfirst into any of the crazed. He couldn't look at his surroundings. If he saw someone in distress, he didn't trust himself. It was in his very nature to save them.

As they rode, Alayna inched her scooter next to his, peering at him with questioning eyes. Clay called over the motor, "What is it?"

"Something's wrong," she said. Her eyes surveyed the string of empty buildings they passed.

"What do you mean? It's just been evacuated, I'm sure," Clay said. "I don't think that's cause for alarm."

"Sure," Alayna said, then countered, "But Helen is twice the size of Carterville. There's bound to be someone around. Someone like us—" She swallowed sharply. "I mean, admit it, Clay. We haven't seen anyone, either alive or dead. Bodies. You know it's true."

Clay slowed his moped, allowing Ralph and Brandon to buzz past them. Daniels brought up the rear, his gun strapped across his lap. His eyes darted side to side, looking for threats.

Clay said, "I, for one, am savoring this solitude. We're on bikes. We can get away from the crazed as soon as we see them. This is about as invincible as we're going to be, maybe for a very long time. Just enjoy it, Alayna."

She didn't respond. Jacobs slowed on Main Street, stopping at a storefront with the name "Curley's" stenciled on the glass. The name was in red cursive lettering that was strangely ominous, like a candy shop from the 1950s.

The rest pulled up and parked in a line behind Jacob's bike. In the window, Clay scrutinized their reflections: mangy heads and battered bodies, the setting sun as a backdrop.

"Hey," Clay exclaimed. "Isn't the candy store in Carterville called Moe's?"

"Yeah, that's right," Jacobs replied.

Clay almost laughed. "Let me guess, there's a candy store called Larry's around somewhere, too?"

"As a matter of fact, our Larry's storefront is about a hundred miles from here," Jacobs agreed. "It's another lab, just like this one."

Ralph cackled madly. "Jesus Christ. Moe, Larry, and Curley. You have got to be kidding me," he roared. "What is this? I hope I wake up soon. This has been the longest dream of my life."

Alayna didn't laugh, but her eyes twinkled, she got the joke. Jacobs reached up and scratched his forehead, aware he was out of the loop. Still cackling, Ralph tapped his shoulder. "Don't worry too much, kid. You just have some catching up to do, don't you? But who knows if we'll ever find a television that works so you can watch it."

"Watch what?" Jacobs asked.

Clay stopped laughing to stare at Jacobs, incredulous. "You mean, you've been working in these labs, and you don't know?"

"The Moe, Larry, and Curley labs? Yes," Jacobs said. His eyebrows drew together and he stiffened, resentful.

"Oh, Leland. It's not that big of a deal," Ralph said, hopping from his moped in an oddly childlike movement. "Just a bit of silly television from a different time. You were probably too busy in the lab your whole life to have that much fun. All you have to know is this: The Three Stooges were the greatest cultural icons ever. Period."

Alayna winked at Jacobs. "I think you probably used your life a lot better. Learning. Seeing. Doing. Not wasting it away in front of the boob tube, like us."

"I thought they were great," Daniels said.

The others gaped at him, surprised at his joyful smile. They all laughed and began up the steps of the candy store. The moment of relief was welcome, their tension faded a degree. Clay patted Jacobs on the back, telling him, "Thanks for getting us here. You're a first-rate guide, Leland. I'm sorry I ever doubted you."

Jacobs placed his palm firmly against the door and pushed it open. The sales floor was abandoned, shadowy, with containers of candy still on display. Gumballs gleamed in the soft, sunset light, licorice swirls in knots in a massive jar. Brandon reached into a container of gummy bears, pulling out a big handful and munching it. Alayna smacked his hand, shaking her head. "You're going to get a cavity, and we haven't met a dentist yet."

"If I die, I want to go out eating candy," Brandon insisted. "I don't know how many times I have to tell you that, but I'll keep doing it." He reached back into the container, grabbing more. "Besides, they're delicious." He handed a few to her, placing them delicately in her outstretched palm. She ripped the head off a green bear with her front teeth, closing her eyes and chewing.

"See? I told you," Brandon said smugly.

"Shhh," Jacobs said. He turned toward the back of the store. It was nearly identical to the one in Carterville, with a door that led to the downstairs lab. He went toward it tentatively.

"Are they back there?" Daniels whispered.

"I can't tell," Jacobs said.

There was a loud bang on the other side of the door. Alayna jumped, nearly choking on her gummies. Jacobs froze. Clay bolted up beside him, ready to fight. He scanned the room. "What was that?"

Another bang echoed through the store.

Candy jars began to crash down from the higher shelves, scattering glass shards across the floor. Everyone leaped back, except for Daniels. He rushed ahead, slipping a pair of sunglasses over his eyes for protection. He drove toward the back door, which was now standing wide open. He didn't hesitate before disappearing into the darkness.

Moments later, Daniels cried out. A net had dropped over his head, and he flailed wildly, his thick arms protruding through the net, but unable to free himself.

Broomsticks and bats, seemingly of their own volition, began to assault him, knocking him down. Brandon screamed before Alayna dragged him away from the chaos.

Something connected with Daniels' face, shattering his sunglasses. The blows rained mercilessly, leaving him unable to speak.

"JESUS CHRIST! STOP IT!" Alayna screamed. Clay wasn't sure if they should turn back and leave Daniels at the mercy of these monsters. He froze with indecision. The seconds ticked on.

9.

Finally, Clay shook off his hesitation. He drew his gun and sprinted toward Daniels. As he skidded to a stop he felt a bat slam into his forearm, knocking his gun to the floor. He thrust his hand out and caught the bat mid-swing. He strained, pulling the bat upward and away from the assailant and caught a glimpse of the person who held it

He shouted, "WE AREN'T THE MONSTERS! WE'RE HUMAN! STOP THIS!"

It took several moments for the woman to give up the bat. She was black-haired and wide-eyed behind old-fashioned, horn-rimmed glasses. She was standing with another woman, blonde and similarly bug-eyed, still unwilling to give up her broom handle.

"LADIES! PLEASE! WE'RE NOT THE CRAZED! HEY!"

Clay ripped the broom from her hands, and tossed both weapons behind him. The women slowly came out of their hiding places. They blinked at him, confused by his presence.

"Hello?" the black-haired one said. "Jesus. Sorry. We aren't used to humans. I mean—we've only seen each other for . . ." her voice trailed off.

The silence hung between them. Daniels was still tangled in the net, struggling to get free. He grunted angrily.

"Can you guys give me a hand?"

Clay helped extricate him, then helped him back to his feet. Daniels brushed himself off, glaring at the blonde woman. "What do I look like to you?"

"We said we're sorry," she whimpered.

"Who are you, anyway?" the black-haired woman asked. "You have quite a group here."

After a short pause, Jacobs stepped forward. "Marcia," he said, his voice soft. "It's me. Leland."

Marcia's jaw dropped in disbelief. "What the hell?" she gasped as she pushed between Daniels and Clay, then wrapped her arms tightly around Jacobs' neck. The other woman followed closely, joining them in an intimate hug: three scientists, united at the laboratory, after destroying the rest of the world.

Clay tried to remind himself to stay calm and not think of it that way. In the end, no matter whose fault it was, they were now part of an exclusive group of survivors. He had to stay strong, leader-like. He lifted his chin, and looked toward Alayna. Her eyes reflected similar thoughts and feelings.

"I can't believe you're alive," Marcia whispered, tears trickling down her cheeks. "We didn't think you'd make it. We heard—" she trailed off, unsure how to finish.

"We were worried, is all," the other woman said. She was prim, less emotional. She righted herself, even as Marcia clung to Jacobs like he was a long-lost brother, or even a lover.

"Well, I did," Jacobs said. His face twisted slightly. Clay eyed him suspiciously, remembering how they'd found him at the lab all alone. Jacobs made eye contact with Marcia, communicating a thousand different emotions.

"What is it, Leland?" She asked. "Just say what's on your mind."

Jacobs swallowed. The weight of what he'd just been through seemed to come back to him "I haven't been able to come to terms with the fact that you left me there," he said. "You knew this was all going to happen. We shouldn't have split up—"

"Listen, guys?" Alayna said, scanning the darkening street through the window. "I appreciate that you have a lot to talk about. But we should move this to the lab. Who knows what's out there."

The scientists led everyone into the lab and then sealed the door, locking them in. The reinforced walls made them feel safe, albeit momentarily. Daniels, still anxious from being trapped, stood at the door, his finger tapping the barrel of his gun. Safety was never a given.

10.

The survivors entered the first anteroom of the whitewashed lab. The two resident scientists, who were introduced as Lane Burke and Marcia Wright, disappeared for a few minutes to get water bottles. They passed them around wordlessly, and watched as the dirt-smudged clan drank thirstily. Marcia caressed Jacobs' shoulder, rubbing at his tense muscles. It was clear that she was dismayed at how horrendous they all looked.

"Did you walk all the way from Carterville?" she asked incredulously.

"Ha. We tried to drive," Daniels replied, still angry at the ambush. "But the minute we went through a gap in the force field, the damn thing came back on again."

Marcia brought her hand to her mouth, clearly shocked. "Jesus. And you survived?"

"Miraculously, we've only suffered a few bumps and bruises," Alayna said, giving Ralph reassuring smile.

"Well, you shouldn't have lived through that," Marcia said softly. "It's remarkable you did. It shows incredible courage."

The survivors didn't bother to answer. Their minds were numb. But Clay had questions, and the two scientists had the answers.

"Why didn't you take Leland with you?" Clay asked, setting his empty water bottle on a desk. He crossed his arms over his chest, like a parent waiting for a childish excuse.

Lane spun toward Clay, an apology on her lips. "It was that woman. Lois Washington."

"The mayor?" Alayna asked warily.

"Yes. She told us to move to Helen, a week before the outbreak," Lane explained.

"Jesus. Lois knew about this? She—she knew, and then used that . . . asteroid as a cover-up . . ." Clay stammered, leaning heavily against a desk.

Lois had been his boss for years; a woman he and the rest of the town of Carterville had turned to for support and reassurance. He remembered her glittering, eagle eyes, her fine features. How could such deceit lurk behind her facade?

"That's right," Lane agreed. "She definitely knew about the DoD project."

"But that's not all." Marcia continued, "Once they arrived here in Helen, she and Colonel Wallace began to separate those who were showing symptoms from healthy people. They knew it was going to get worse, and they were trying to get ahead of it. Kind of like, say, concentration camps. From World War II."

"Jesus," Clay whispered. "What did they do with them?"

"First off, they rounded up anyone confirmed to have the infection, what was the term you used?" Lane asked.

"The crazed," Clay replied.

"Well, that sounds appropriate. They put all the crazed in the back of large container trucks and sent them south, toward Dearing I think," Marcia said. "Then, anyone starting to show symptoms, but hadn't turned yet. Those who seemed to have no hope, well, they sent them south too. Not sure where, though."

"Most likely to Dearing," Lane said.

"And what about the others? The people with no symptoms?" Alayna asked, hopeful. "Where'd they go?"

"They were sent north. To a military base, up near Earlton," Lane said.

Clay and Alayna glanced at each other, both realizing that they might have just discovered the answer to where Megan, Valerie, and Maia were.

"Do you—do you know anything about a girl named Megan?" Alayna asked then. "Megan Holt? She's beautiful, a resident of Carterville, around my age—"

Marcia and Lane shook their heads sadly.

"What about my family?" Clay asked. "Valerie and Maia Dobbs. A teenage girl with a woman around my age. Did you see anyone like that?"

"We mostly kept to the lab," Lane said quietly, her eyes dropping to the ground. "We didn't want to risk being contaminated ourselves. Plus, we couldn't be shipped off to the military base."

"Not even for your safety?" Alayna asked.

"There's no telling if it's safer than here," Marcia said. "This a global catastrophe. All the rules are out the window. We have to make it up as we go along."

"Wait—" Clay said, raising a finger. The voicemails from Valerie were never far from his mind. "I received a call from my wife. She was here, in Helen. She said that she and our daughter were split up, and that our daughter might have the flu."

After a pause, Lane said, "Sounds about right. That's why they were separated, then. The people with flu-like symptoms went south. And your wife, well, it sounds like she went north."

"Jesus," Clay gasped, sinking into a chair. His stomach churned with anxiety. His baby. His Maia. She was alone, trapped, maybe warding off other crazed monsters all the way down in Dearborn. His shoulders began to shake.

All the way to Helen, he'd clung to this hope: that he'd learn his daughter and wife's whereabouts when he arrived. But he hadn't expected such devastating news. Not after he'd been through so much already.

11.

C lay erupted from his chair, pushed past Daniels and unlatched the door. His thoughts were churning with panic and despair. He needed to go, run, find his family. There were tears on his cheeks. Tears of anger at Lois Washington, the woman who was supposed to protect them. And of anger at himself. He'd stayed behind, to help in Carterville. He should have gone with Valerie and Maia. Carterville was no more, most of its residents were either crazed or dead.

And he still couldn't be certain about Maia and Valerie.

"Fuck," Clay shouted, darting out the door. Daniels snagged Clay's jacket, yanking him back. "Let me go, Adam!" he cried. "I've got to get out." He began to hyperventilate. "Jesus Christ. Just let go of me. Haven't I done enough?"

But Daniels held Clay firmly and slammed the door shut. Clay dropped to his knees, suddenly exhausted. He searched for any meaning in all of this.

Alayna bent down in front of him and cupped his cheeks. Her hands were cool, and oddly soothing.

"Shh," she whispered. "You can't do this. You'll destroy yourself. Mentally—emotionally—physically.

And we need you, Clay."

The other survivors formed a half-circle around them, looking down anxiously, their eyes brimming with worry and dust from the road.

"I want to run out there, too," Alayna said. "I want to find Megan just as much as you want to find your family. But without something to go on—without a plan—it might very well be suicide."

"So, you want to give up?" Clay said, his voice raspy. "Because it might be unsafe out there?"

"No. We're going to stay here long enough to replenish our supplies, find more ammunition, and, most of all, rest, Clay," Alayna said in a quiet voice.

"We don't really know what's beyond Helen, anyway," Marcia interjected. "We know Helen's safe. There aren't many of the crazed, just a few that get past the military's perimeter. But leaving without being prepared would be foolish."

"I agree," Lane said, her eyes sympathetic. "And I'm sorry. I really am." She shrugged her thin shoulders, dwarfed by her massive lab coat.

Jacobs pointed to another room, which held most of the lab's equipment. A blue light was strobing, casting flickering shadows. "What experiments could you possibly by doing right now, anyway?" he asked.

Marcia and Lane exchanged a look. Clay stood. His cheeks were flushed, with panic and with shame. He pushed his hair back, grateful it was no longer thinning like it had been a few weeks before. He'd kept up with the medication for radiation poisoning, reducing his symptoms.

"Well, I suppose they'll have to see it at some point," Marcia began, speaking to Lane.

"The back rooms are where we keep the supplies.

The food. The beds," Lane said, her eyes flashing. "But you'll have to walk past our most recent round of experiments. And you might want to hold your breath. Especially if you have a weak stomach."

Ralph said, "Lady, we've been out there murdering these monsters right and left. I don't think I'll ever get their stench out of my coat." He lifted his stump. "I even shot my best friend, on accident. But, we're closer because of it. I don't think we'll be alarmed by any little hoity-toity experiment you're doing in here."

Clay stifled laughter. Alayna pressed her lips together. Lane led them into the second room, past the blue light. On the tables, the survivors witnessed a disgusting sight. Something they weren't ready for, despite the warnings.

Crazed humans were restrained on tables, a number of them partially vivisected. Their greying hearts and lungs were exposed to the light, glistening horribly. Some had their arms cut off, others no longer had legs. Across the room, jars holding assorted organs were scattered on a table.

Alayna covered her mouth and nose, trying to block out the stench. Ralph and Brandon both turned away. Clay was trying not to look at the faces of the crazed humans, knowing there was a chance he might recognize any one of them. If they'd come up from Carterville, he might very well find an ex-neighbor or an old friend.

Jacobs, however, showed intense interest. He walked around the bodies, skimming the notes about each one. "I see," he murmured. "You were trying to get to the cause of the infection."

"That's right," Lane said. She was clearly acclimated to the stench. A part of her everyday routine. "We ran just about every test that we could think of. Took volumes of blood samples. Looked at their stool samples."

"We even studied their dental progressions," Marcia said. "It appears their mouths completely change after their transformation."

"Fascinating," Jacobs whispered. He snapped latex gloves on his hands, and pushed open a crazed woman's mouth. He peered in, his eyes widening. "Jesus. She almost has fangs—"

"That's right," Lane sounded oddly excited. "But we haven't been successful in finding a cause, or a cure, unfortunately. It seems to be irreversible."

"Well, I'm here now," Jacobs said, his eyes intense. "There's bound to be something you haven't thought of. Something we can test for . . ." He trailed off, his mind humming. Marcia and Lane joined him near the body, leaving the rest hovering against the wall, wishing for a way out.

Brandon joined Clay, his eyes watery. "Dude. She said Helen's clear of the monsters, right?"

Nonplussed by Jacobs' reaction to the experiments, Clay nodded. "Yeah, she did," he said.

"Well, then, let's get the fuck out of here," Brandon said. "Let's find something real to eat."

"I think we should stay down here," Clay said hesitantly. "They said they have food down here—"

But Brandon objected. "No. I don't want to eat another goddamned granola bar. I want something real and hot and good. There's bound to be a place around here that's stocked up. You know, the way the Carterville hotel was."

Clay tore his eyes away from the scientist and looked at his companions, noting that they were all stooped, their eyes dark and hollow. They were clearly malnourished, they'd left the hotel some time ago. He cleared his throat.

"Gang?" he said. "Let's go find some grub."

Lane gave him a warm smile. She broke off her scientific, lab-talk, and pointed toward the door. "You know, there's a great café across the street."

Brandon's smile widened, showing his candy-coated teeth. "You heard the woman, Clay," he said. "I'm going to eat at that café if it's the last thing I do."

Clay patted his back and followed him up the steps and out into the darkness. When the door of the candy shop closed behind them, everyone— including the scientists—inhaled the fresh mountain air deeply, grateful to leave the putrid stench behind.

12.

The café was a local place, not a franchise, with diner-like booths, different colored lamps on the walls, and a long, thin mirror wrapping around the dining room. Clay felt immediately at home there, reminded of all the dinners he'd had with his wife and daughter at the Carterville diner. Maia always ordered a grilled cheese, his wife, a burger, choosing to nibble both his and Maia's fries. He shivered at the memory, suddenly craving a massive meal.

Brandon and Ralph bolted for the kitchen, with the scientists following close behind. Clay heard Ralph muttering something about biscuits and gravy, as it was easy, and could fill up the whole troop.

Clay followed a moment later, finding the two scientists looking stunned. "Why didn't we ever think to make that?" Lane joked, tapping Ralph on the back.

Marcia laughed. "We needed people around. Otherwise, we were going to keep eating the same four things until we died."

The survivors helped each other, with Ralph running the show. He made homemade biscuits, using whole-grain flour and stirring with his left hand, impressing everyone with his one-handed skills. One of the scientists flipped on the radio. They heard music for the first time in what felt like years. It was an '80s song, one from Clay's youth. He closed his eyes and leaned back against a cabinet, remembering Valerie whistling the tune to herself as she drove in the car.

Would he ever hear her melody again?

Thirty minutes later, Brandon and Daniels shoved several tables together and set out silverware. Alayna collected some fake flowers from the back and arranged them in coffee cups, dotting them between the plates. Ralph brought out a vat of sausage gravy, and Jacobs followed him out with a large tray of biscuits. They portioned out the meal quickly, and then everyone sat, almost in awe at how delicious their impromptu meal really looked. They felt like they were outside of time, like travelers from the future, looking at a distant past.

"What are you waiting for?" Ralph said. "Prayer? Because you can wait all night for that. I'm not going to give it to you."

They ate then, ripping open their biscuits and dipping them into the gravy, slathering still more over their plates. As they ate, the lights flickered around them, a reminder of the power outages in Carterville.

Clay pointed his knife in the air. "You've been getting these too?" he asked.

Lane nodded slowly, taking a small bite. "In fact, we need to tell you that it's really messing with the meat and dairy. We thought we'd have this stuff for a while longer, but as Ralph was cooking it—"

"Oh, yeah," Ralph said, interrupting. "This shit only has a few more days, if that. But it's good for now, ain't it?"

"Good for now?" Brandon said nervously, eyeing his half-eaten meal. "I'm not going to get sick, am I? I got food poisoning once. On a trip to Florida. I was over the toilet for hours."

Marcia reassured him, "If it was going to make you sick, it would have happened before you'd eaten half your plate."

"We've moved quite a bit of the frozen food to the freezer in the lab. But we might have to say goodbye to meat and dairy. At least for a while," Lane said quietly.

Silence fell. They listened to the unfamiliar sound of each other chewing vigorously, reveling in flavor of meat and fat and bone-sticking goodness. Finally, Clay cleared his throat, dropping his fork back on his plate.

"There's something wrong with you, isn't there?" Lane asked.

The rest of the survivors turned toward Clay, alarm in their eyes. Brandon quit eating immediately, and covered his mouth. "It's this fucking meat, isn't it?" he asked. "I knew I shouldn't—"

But Lane held up a finger, stopping him. "You guys haven't noticed how pale this man is?" she asked.

Alayna assessed Clay from the other side of the table. "I assumed it was stress."

"It's hard to know if any of us look right," Daniels chimed in. "We're all on the brink of insanity, aren't we?"

Clay sensed she could almost smell the radiation poisoning inside him. Disgruntled, he pulled himself to his feet and began to pace, the savory flavor of the meal still coating his tongue. Everyone was staring, and no one was eating any longer.

"What's the story, Clay?" Lane asked in a gentle voice.

"He wasn't infected, was he?" Marcia asked, looking at Jacobs.

Jacobs shook his head, his movements almost imperceptible. "My preliminary analysis," he began, his voice cracking, "is that Clay has radiation poisoning. From the meteorite."

The scientists' faces were grim. The other survivors seemed to be seeing Clay for the first time. Alayna burst from her chair and wrapped her arms around him, hugging him tight.

"How much time do you think I have?" Clay asked. He scratched the back of his neck, remembering how weak he'd been before Jacobs had started giving him the pills. "Oddly enough, I feel stronger now than I did before. Much more . . . aware, even. It's like those pills are making me a better version of myself, despite being generally malnourished and exhausted. Does that align with the diagnosis?"

Alayna nodded, her eyebrows furrowing. "You do look better than you have for the past few days," she said slowly. "I didn't want to say anything. I just thought you were stressed out." She shrugged, not wanting to comment on the fact that they hadn't really been speaking, not since they'd slept together.

"So, he's cured?" Ralph said, taking a large bite of biscuits and gravy, the first to return to his food.

"It's too early to tell," Jacobs said.

"And you're sure you didn't have any recent contact with one of the crazed?" Marcia asked. "I was watching you earlier. You were sweating in the kitchen. Like you have a fever." She paused. "That is a symptom of the infection."

Clay's mind filled with those first images of Cliff in the jail cell, sweating and weeping and vomiting, fighting what Clay had assumed was a hangover. God, he'd been so wrong.

"The first guy was Cliff," he told them. "The guy you said worked in the lab. I was fighting him off, right after he became completely—out of it." He remembered the volatile motions, the insane eyes. "And as we were fighting, I got some of his blood in my mouth—" He stopped, allowing the information to sink in.

Both Marcia and Lane were shocked. They pushed their chairs back.

"Now, don't jump to conclusions," Jacobs said to them. "He's been with us for a while now and he doesn't have any of the symptoms. If he was going to turn crazed, he would have already."

"So it's radiation poisoning?" Lane asked. "There's no way to know the truth, Leland. Not until we test him."

Clay shook his head. Rather than race after his wife and daughter, he would be confined in a lab, tested, "discovered." He glared at Jacobs, and wanted to insist on a better tactic, on any other plan.

But Jacobs nodded his head slowly. "It won't take long, Clay. And it'll give you the answers you're looking for. You need to do this. If you don't, you could drop dead in the middle of your search. And all this will have been for nothing."

Clay picked up his plate of biscuits and gravy. He felt like smashing the plate, watching the shards rain all over the diner. But his friends were searching his face, waiting for his answer.

He set the plate down in front of Brandon, their "child," their growing boy. "Eat up, kid," he said. He turned back toward Jacobs. "All right. Let's get this over with, then," he said gruffly.

Clay stormed out onto the deserted street, feeling desolation and loneliness quiver in his soul. If he didn't survive this, he knew Valerie and Maia wouldn't, either.

13.

C lay stood, half-naked, his skin scrubbed clean and his toes bare for the first time in weeks. His toenails were cracked and yellow from all the walking. Lane, Jacobs, and Marcia had worked on him for over thirty minutes, taking blood, saliva, and urine samples to assess his overall health.

As Clay stood there, he looked down, assessing his muscled body. Since they'd taken to fighting the crazed tooth-and-nail, he'd suffered several injuries. He'd been knocked to the ground by their incredible strength, causing cuts and bruises. Once, he'd fallen on his knife, before he'd lurched back up, gasping, with blood on his shirt. He'd just bandaged the wound afterward, hoping it wasn't as deep as it had felt.

Of course, once your body took on so much pain, it was easy to forget the minute details, the tiny scrapes. You trudged forward, day after night after day, becoming one with your pain. He often remembered Maia who, when she fell off her bicycle and scraped her elbow, refused to ever get back on to ride again.

If he was going to follow the metaphor, he and the other survivors had fallen off their bikes, gotten hit by three semi-trucks, and then proceeded to vomit uncontrollably, while still finding the will to keep going.

He hoped Maia had found some kind of commitment to life, out there on her own.

But all the wounds—minor or otherwise—all seemed to be healing incredibly fast. Clay bent over, unnoticed by the busy scientists, and assessed the knife wound. It had completely scabbed over in a few days, despite its depth. The bruises on his knees were returning to normal color, and the scrapes and cuts were basically gone. Clay tilted his head, confused.

"Hey. I have a question," he said, his voice cracking slightly.

Jacobs whirled around, still used to Clay being his quasi-leader. "What is it?"

"All these injuries. They're healing really fast," Clay said, gesturing at his naked legs. "Normally, it's not this fast. Is that a side effect of radiation poisoning? Fast healing?"

The scientists exchanged glances. In the back room, he could hear Ralph and Brandon joking with each other, playing a game in which they tossed gummy bears into one another's mouths. He'd seen Brandon wincing an hour before, when something had irritated his gunshot wound. But, as Clay had said at dinner, he was feeling stronger, more athletic, closer to rational thinking. Why? Could there be an actual, scientific explanation?

Could these scientists actually prove to be useful?

"We don't have a lot of experience in this field," Lane began, sounding tentative. "Radiation isn't our area of expertise. But we do know that radiation poisoning generally doesn't have any healing properties."

"Not at all," Marcia said, her words insistent. "Your body should be dying. You should be on the ground, writhing in pain. But you're living, you're surviving, and you're healing."

Jacobs considered that. But before he could speak, Lane gasped, gesturing at the lab results in front of her. Clay's heart sank, sure he was about to receive horrible news.

He wasn't wrong. But he wasn't actually right, either.

"Jesus. Okay. I have good news, and bad," Lane said, sounding jittery. She was poised over her computer, which was spitting the lab results in a long stream of information.

"I don't know how to take that." Clay laughed nervously. He felt naked and strange in front of them, his toes gripping the cold tile floor.

"The good news is that you've been exposed to radiation for a considerable amount of time," Lane said, her eyebrows furrowed with concentration.

"How the hell is that good news?" Clay asked.

"Well, because your body seems to be healing itself despite that exposure," Lane said. "Last week, you were probably feeling the effects of the radiation a great deal—"

"I lost so much of my hair. And I was vomiting uncontrollably," Clay offered.

"Right. But now, your body is bouncing back from that. You're going to live through the radiation. That's something not a lot of people can say," she said. As she spoke, her smile faltered.

"All right," Clay said, his heart speeding up. "Out with the bad news, then. Is it chicken pox? Tell me it's not chicken pox."

None of the scientists laughed at his joke. They studied the information on the screen. After several minutes of tension, Jacobs looked up and told Clay the truth.

"The nanites are present in your blood," he said flatly.

Clay collapsed against the wall behind him. Was this a death sentence? He began to stutter, trying to find reason.

"Th—then I—I need to get the fuck out of here," he said. "I need to get away from all of you. I don't want to hurt anyone—"

But Lane held up her hand, her face stern. "Clay, there's no reason to panic. Not yet, at least. It seems that the nanites are working quite differently in your body than what we've experienced to date."

"How can you tell?" Clay asked, rubbing his hand on his growing beard.

Lane gestured toward the putrid-smelling bodies, splayed out, covered in key places with towels. "Well, we only have your blood to compare with theirs, I suppose," she said. "But your reaction to the nanites is strange. You said it yourself. You were exposed to Cliff's blood several weeks ago, right?"

"Seems like forever," Clay murmured. "But yes. I'm almost certain I was exposed then."

"Right," Lane said. "We need to do more tests. We don't have enough information."

"And how do you expect we'll get that, without getting killed first?" Clay asked, crossing his arms stiffly over his chest.

"Oh, come on, Clay," Jacobs said, almost taunting him. "I've watched your fighting techniques every day since you found me at the lab. They're top-notch. There's no reason you can't go outside of town, grab a crazed, and bring him back here for testing. If we know more about them, we know more about you. Get it?"

Clay frowned. He felt that they were wasting time. Time he needed to find his daughter and his wife. "What do you ladies think?"

"It's dangerous, sure," Marcia said. "And from your stories about their fighting techniques, it seems they're advancing quite rapidly. Unpredictable. When they first transitioned, they'd just flail their arms and try to eat you."

"But from what you've said, it seems they work in packs now. They won't let one of their own go easy. I can't say for sure," Lane finished.

"Why not use the neutralizing device, then?" Marcia said. "They're right over there, just waiting for this kind of problem. Jesus, Lane. I don't know why you didn't think of it before."

Lane blushed and looked at the floor. Suddenly, Jacobs threw a pipette onto the ground, smashing it. Clay leaped back, conscious of his toes.

What the hell was going on?

14.

"You assholes! You just took them," Jacobs spewed, his eyes flashing like a tiger's. "You grabbed the neutralizers, and you just walked out the door. Just like that. You left Cliff and me to die."

Marcia's looked grim. Lane took several steps back, trying to find anything else to look at.

"Do either of you have an explanation? Do either of you want to confess that you could have been responsible for my death? That's murder, ladies," Jacobs continued, crunching through the glass.

"Cliff was an asshole, anyway. He got into the nanites! He didn't know what he was doing," Marcia argued.

"Are you saying it's better that he died?" Jacobs asked, his eyes bulging. "Because I don't think that's very ethical. Do you, Marcia? Lane?"

No one spoke for a moment. Clay reached for his pants, hanging from a lab chair. He stepped into them quickly, cinching them closed at his waist. The scientists turned toward him, almost shocked to see another face in the room.

"You need to stop fighting. Now," Clay said, his voice firm. He straightened up, towering a full six inches over Jacobs, and ten or twelve over the women. He dwarfed them. "It doesn't matter what happened in the past, in Carterville. Trust me. I wish we could go back and fix all the mistakes we made back there. But we can't. And now, my life completely and totally depends on whether or not you three can fix this nanite and radiation debacle in my body. Because if you decide to squabble for the rest of our time here—on Earth, not just in this lab—then I'll surely die."

The scientists didn't speak, didn't even have the strength to argue. He turned his attention to his naked toes, wondering what the future—all their futures—held.

"Am I going to turn into one of them?" he asked, his voice quiet. "Just tell me."

After a long moment of silence, Lane stepped forward. She pulled her glasses from her nose, blinking rapidly. "We're not sure. We're really not, Clay. So, you have to trust us, okay? We're all going to have to figure this out together."

"As far as we know," Jacobs said, "you're the only living, breathing human being that hasn't succumbed to the ravages of the nanites." He reached for a broom, and began to clean the aftermath of his outburst, sweeping the glass shards into a dustbin. They glinted beneath the bright, laboratory light.

"It's actually quite the opposite," Lane said, pointing at the computer screen as if it explained everything. "The nanites seem to be rebuilding you. From the inside out. We don't really know why, or how. But you're alive, Clay. You have to thank your lucky stars for that."

"Ha," Clay blurted.

"That's why you're feeling stronger all the time," Lane said, talking over his sarcasm. "You said that.

It's real, Clay. This is unforeseen science. And it's changing everything we thought we knew."

Clay was silent for a moment. "Do you think I should take any kind of medicine?" he asked. "Anything to slow the nanite production?"

"I propose we leave them for a while," Jacobs said. "We'll monitor your status, of course. We'll make sure nothing changes, and that you maintain this health. For all we know, it could turn on a dime."

"Right," Clay said. He was facing the truth, head-on. He couldn't look weak. Then, something that Marcia said came back to him. "What about these devices? The neutralizing thing? How can they help us?"

"The devices were used to control the soldiers during the early experiments, when we still had control of the nanites," Marcia explained. "There's a possibility that we can adapt these neutralizers and use them to stop the crazed entirely."

"But that's a long, long time from now," Lane said looking hesitant. "We haven't even used them since the outbreak. Or experimented with them since those initial trials."

"But in theory, it would work like this," Marcia said, leaning forward. "The nanites still appear to have their radio frequencies activated. Using a modified version of the neutralizers, we should be able to change the nanites. Destroy them. Kill the crazed from the inside, out."

"Shit. So, that's why you took them from the storage locker?" Jacobs asked, incredulous. "I didn't see any of this. But now—it's so clear—" He leaned back, clearly deep in thought. "The radio waves . . ."

"Right. Precisely," Lane said. "The neutralizers use radio waves, and can ultimately stop the nanites in their tracks, thus destroying the monsters."

"Can't we just use the neutralizers to stop the nanites in my body, then?" Clay asked hopefully. "I'm clearly overriding them, or is the other way around? Anyway, they haven't affected me the way they affected the others, right? Isn't that what you said?"

"Yes, that's right. But there's no way to be sure just how the neutralizer will affect you," Marcia said. "From what we've learned, these nanites—the ones that have mutated somehow—they take over the human host in a way we haven't quite grasped. Stopping them now could potentially kill you."

Clay considered that, realizing that the single thing that could help restore humanity was the very thing that could destroy him. He shifted his weight, his stomach churning with panic, wanting to revolt against the biscuits and gravy.

"This means I shouldn't even be around the device if it's activated?" Clay asked.

The scientists all looked thoughtful. Lane began to shake her head vehemently at Jacobs. But he ignored her. "Not necessarily," he said. "I think we can adapt the transmitter to filter out the unique signature of your strain. As the nanites enter the human host, they take on and adapt to the host. It's almost like they create their own DNA strand, really. And we should be able to filter your particular DNA out of the broadcast, allowing you to personally pull the trigger on the device. Safely. The crazed should drop without affecting you. Theoretically."

Silence fell. Clay's mind raced with all the things that could go wrong if the neutralizer didn't work correctly. Would he feel the nanites dying, before he, too, went down? Should he just give up? He remembered the defeat in Ralph's eyes, and he understood it now.

Lane gripped his shoulder, her eyes wide. "You have to believe we'll do everything in our power to keep you alive, Clay. It's remarkable you're even still here with us."

"And I think the first step," said Marcia, "is to find a host to test the neutralizer on, before testing it on Clay. Someone is going to have to head out, grab a crazed, and bring it back here. And we need to do it soon."

Clay turned on his heel and walked barefoot into the next room, where his friends were. Alayna was watching listlessly as Ralph and Brandon continued to bond. She assessed Clay nervously. They'd all had showers since they'd come back, and they looked like new people, freshly born.

Clay stood beside her, his arms at his sides. He wanted to tell her he could die, he wanted to tell her it might be over soon, and that she'd have to lead the charge. But instead, he just enjoyed the soft scent of her skin, remembering the intimate moments they'd shared. He'd betrayed Valerie, but at least he'd been alive. He'd been happy. He'd felt things. Wasn't that all this world was for?

15.

As the days crept by, the survivors grew more accustomed to Helen. They walked down the streets, fearless, their guns holstered and untouched, knowing that the crazed had been shipped off. This was their sanctuary. More and more, it was feeling like home.

The neutralizers had been completely reprogrammed, with Lane, Marcia, and Leland working tirelessly in their morbid laboratory. Clay eyed them nervously as they worked, wondering if they'd gotten his DNA correct. If they'd miscalculated at all, Clay's death was inevitable.

Finding a crazed to test on was proving difficult, especially given that the survivors had taken such a liking to the town, to regular meals, and to resting their feet.

The day before they were going to leave Helen and expand their hunt for a crazed, Ralph awoke, suddenly unable to remember where he was. He eased his feet over the side of the bed, listening to his knees creak. He tried to push off the bed and stand, but his right hand was missing, and he fell back to the bed.

It was a sudden, horrible reminder of everything that had happened. Connie no longer slept beside him. He had just one hand, and countless bruises and cuts, all from this horrible End of Times. He should have listened to Connie and gone to church more often. But now he didn't feel the depths of any "soul" within him. He just felt tired.

And he needed a drink, dammit. It had been too long.

As he dressed into the same clothes he'd been wearing for what seemed like years, he eyed Brandon's sleeping form near the corner. His heart softened. Brandon was the one good thing to come out of all of this: a boy that was quickly turning into a young man, who'd shown compassion toward an old asshole like him. The kid didn't have a father, a mother, or a sister anymore, and in a way, Ralph was his only family.

Should he wake him up? Ralph wondered. Should he tell him he was going for a walk, that he needed company? Brandon looked peaceful, his eyes moving behind the lids, dreaming. If Ralph had ever had a son, he imagined he would be like Brandon. Silly at times, but with a good head on his shoulders.

Ralph slipped his boots on before retreating through the laboratory, past the stinking corpses and into the brightly lit candy shop. He grabbed a few gummies, along with a grenade for protection, as he left, chewing on the gummies ravenously. In this new life, he was always hungry. He skulked through the empty streets, watching the sun began to rise, casting long shadows on the pavement.

Ralph passed the café, rounding the corner toward a local bar called Mel's. He'd heard of it, oddly enough. It was a place his own uncle had frequented; he'd become a drunk and died a drunk in Helen.

The door was open, and Ralph entered casually,

like it was his living room. The place was dim and shadowy, several half-full glasses still littering the bar. Cash had been left beneath some of them, showing that people hadn't been here since before they understood that the world was ending and that money made no difference.

Ralph sauntered up to the bar, saying gruffly, "Hey there, Mel." He pulled the dollar bills from beneath the glasses. "It's a busy night in here, isn't it?"

He stretched them out, making eye contact with a stoic George Washington, and then tucked them into his back pocket. He went behind the bar, impressed with the immense selection of whiskey, scotch, and rum. He poured himself a glass of fifty-year-old scotch, leaning heavily against the bar top and sipping. "Mel. You've done some of your best work with this drink," he murmured. The scotch was fire, warming his insides and making his throat sting. But he couldn't care about his organs, his body. Not now. He was just a sack of bones, losing more weight every day. And he wanted to drink himself into a stupor. For old time's sake.

He continued to drink, taking up residence at the bar and occasionally talking to the bartender, and sometimes with Connie. They'd always bickered at their local joint, becoming the couple that everyone came out to watch tear each other to shreds. But god, he'd really loved her. Her flashing tongue, her sultry eyes. She became so much more than who she was when he met her, when she was a girl.

And what had he become? Just the straggler in a tired band of survivors. A drunk who hadn't had a drink in weeks.

He poured himself another, and then another,

enjoying the buzz that started behind his ears and grew around his forehead, his cheeks, his throat. He looked out through the dirty, cigarette-tinged lace curtains from bygone days, and realized it had to be close to noon already. What were the others thinking? he wondered. Would they hunt for him, as they'd hunted for the crazed? Or would they dismiss him as another lost soul in a sea of them?

As he tipped back his sixth drink, he suddenly remembered Brandon. He had to return, soon, if only for the boy's sake. Leaving Brandon alone with the likes of Daniels, that asshole cop Clay, and that prissy lesbian Alayna, didn't sit right with him. He scooted off his stool and grabbed a full bottle of whiskey, thinking he could take sips of it in private, just to take the edge off.

That would help him for a while. It would help him sleep at night.

He stepped out and onto the road, feeling drunk. His eyes stung from the sudden onslaught of sunlight. He turned toward the candy store, unsurprised to see that none of the other survivors were out calling his name. No one really cared about him, right? He'd always known that. He'd been able to lie to himself, for a while. But he wasn't a fool.

He rounded the corner and turned on to Main Street. He stopped to sip whiskey straight from the bottle, noting that someone was standing outside the candy shop, his hands on his slim hips, his eyes scanning the street.

It was the kid. It was Brandon out looking for him.

He stumbled forward, anxious to be reunited with his friend. But as he shuffled forward, a large, huffing man appeared in the doorway of an old apartment building. The monster lunged forward, crashing into Ralph, and forcing him to the ground. Ralph's whiskey bottle went flying and shattered against the pavement. He shrieked like a wild animal, realizing the crazed had him. He had his massive hands around Ralph's neck. And his rotting teeth were mere inches from his scalp.

"BRANDON!" Ralph cried. "BRANDON!"

But before he could call out again, the crazed had latched onto his neck, licking at the blood as it began to gush. Ralph's eyes nearly leaped from his head with panic. He watched, feeling almost outside of his body, as Brandon began to run toward him, drawing his gun.

The chewing grew more insistent. Ralph knew then that it was too late. He was going to succumb to this death. The crazed's tongue was lashing his neck and upper chest, feeling grotesque and snake-like.

Then Ralph remembered. He'd grabbed a grenade from Daniels' vest on the way out of the candy store, just in case. Jesus. He reached down, feeling for it in his pocket.

Before Brandon got to him, he cried out, "NO, STOP! DON'T COME ANY CLOSER, KID!"

Brandon was almost twenty feet away, but Ralph could see his helpless tears.

"IT'S BETTER THIS WAY," Ralph shrieked. "JUST TRUST ME, KID!"

He ripped the pin from the grenade and within seconds exploded into gory shrapnel, arms and legs and blood and organs splattering across the brick walls of the surrounding buildings. The blood was bright red, stark and strange against the blue sky above.

Brandon sank to his knees, feeling the spray of

Ralph's blood on his cheeks. He wiped them off with the back of his sleeve. And then he wailed, his voice echoing against the buildings.

16.

Clay was deep in thought on his lower bunk when Brandon reentered the laboratory, splattered with crimson. His face was sullen and his lips turned down. Without speaking, he collapsed in a chair near his bed, ripping his shirt off, then wiping it across his face to rid it of gunk.

"Jesus, Brandon. What happened?" Clay jumped up.

Brandon began to shake. His eyes darted around the room, unable to focus.

"Brandon," Clay said, placing his hands firmly on the boy's shoulders. "You're going to need to tell me what happened out there. It's no use being catatonic. Let me help you."

Brandon gave him a dark look, a look Clay had seen on Maia's face when he'd demanded she tell him what she was up to. "It's Ralph," he said. "He's fucking dead."

Clay was stunned. Despite all the previous deaths, this still rattled him to the bone. "Tell me what happened."

"I couldn't find him all morning," Brandon said. "And I was worried, because we had plans today. We were going to walk along the edge of town. Near the dump. Searching for crazed, sure, but also rooting around for stuff people might have left behind. Ralph figured there was going to be a resurgence, in time, when gold and silver would mean everything. We wanted to be billionaires when the tide turned."

This sounded like typical Ralph talk, but Clay held his tongue.

"He was on his way back. On the corner, down the road. And one of them got him. He blew himself up with a grenade. And now I have his blood all over me," Brandon whispered. "Jesus. I know we're all going to die, Clay, but this is too fucking much."

"We're not going to die," Clay insisted. "Ralph . . . must have just made a stupid mistake. He knows better than to be out there by himself."

"I should have had his back," Brandon said, beginning to sob. "I was the only person who cared about him. I should have told him that, every day. It think he wanted this to happen. It feels like—"

"You have to stop dwelling on it," Clay said, his voice gruff. "You have to find a way to move on, Brandon. This is a new reality. There are new rules. You can't die out there just because you see no reason to live."

"You don't see a reason," Brandon spat at him, snot starting to run. "Without your wife. Without your daughter. I see you, Clay. You're less of a man because of it. We all see it."

"Yeah, but I'm fighting to live. Every single second, every single hour. I know that they're out there waiting for me, somewhere. And son, I know your family's gone. But you have to find another reason to go on. Your friends from Carterville. You know some of them are still alive. You know they're wondering about you. You know you're not forgotten."

Brandon looked up to where Alayna stood in the doorway. After a long, tension-filled pause, Alayna put her hand on Clay's shoulder, making him jump.

"Clay," she murmured. "Maybe let him be for a bit."

Clay spun toward her and was startled by her face. Her eyes were tinged with red, as if she cried blood of her own. The others were together in the next room, waiting quietly for details about Ralph's death.

They needed Clay's words to console them.

Clay nodded silently then joined the others. He cleared his throat and then suggested they reconvene next door, at the diner, where they could discuss their next steps.

17.

"It's with a heavy heart that I say we must proceed without Ralph," Clay said. "I'm sure you know what happened."

No one looked at him. They drifted from the laboratory, leaving Brandon in the barracks, crying alone. The atmosphere had changed. During the previous days, they'd felt safe, warm, building a sense of normalcy in their fucked-up lives. But now Ralph was plastered all over the courthouse wall, and time was ticking. The crazed were beginning to return to Helen and they couldn't wait for another one to stumble into town and catch them off guard.

In the diner, Daniels and Lane made them toast with jam, and any frozen vegetables they could find. The meat and dairy had gone bad days earlier, leaving them hungry for protein and feeling bleary-eyed and fatigued.

The survivors sat at their familiar booths, chewing sadly on soggy toast. The jam was tart and sweet, making Clay's teeth ache.

Jacobs eyed him curiously from behind his growing beard. After several minutes of silence, he said, "What do you think we should do next, then?"

Clay sighed. "Well, we certainly can't wait here."

"Agreed," Daniels said. "It's just like in

Carterville. If we stay, we die anyway. Forward motion is key."

"You thinking we should go to the military base, then?" Marcia asked. "You said your wife might be there. And that's the best place to take the neutralizers." She took a bite of her toast, scattering crumbs across the table. She brushed them to the ground, knowing no one would mind the mess. Not ever again.

"That's true. I do think one of the neutralizers should go to Earlton," Clay said. "And I think you all should make your way up there to rejoin what's left of our fractured society."

"You all?" Jacobs asked.

"Yes, all of you. I don't want to lose anyone else," Clay said, his voice almost a whisper. Ralph's absence left a hole. Without his raspy jokes, his general air of mischief, a grey stillness filled the room.

"Adam, you'll lead the troop up to the base," Clay said. "You'll all go with him, with one of the neutralizers." He pointed back toward the candy store, remembering Brandon, alone in the dark. "The kid, too. He's been through enough already, and he needs to be with some people his own age. Some people who might understand what he's feeling. I'm sure there are plenty of orphans up at the base. Unfortunately." His eyes flashed.

No one replied. Daniels adjusted himself in his seat, seeming to hold in countless arguments. He wasn't one to miss a fight.

Clay turned toward Alayna and cleared his throat. "Alayna, I think it would be best if you went to Earlton as well. I don't want to endanger you, either. But of course, the decision is up to you."

Alayna's jaw was rigid. She looked hard. Clay knew that her only thoughts were of Megan, her girlfriend and lost love. They were both endlessly romantic, not to mention stubborn. They wouldn't lose their loves without a fight.

"And where on this Earth are *you* planning to go, sheriff?" Alayna asked quietly.

"I have to go after Maia." Saying her name out loud felt bizarre, like he was summoning a ghost. He turned quickly to Lane, who was medically trained, unlike Jacobs and Marcia. "And Lane, I'd like your help on the way there. I don't know what we'll find once we get to Dearing. But your medical know-how could make this expedition successful. Naturally, this is also up to you. I'll do my best to protect you."

Lane's eyes flashed. She turned toward Alayna, and then decided. "I'll do it. I worked as an EMT in grad school."

"And I'm coming with you," Alayna added. "One hundred percent. I won't let my sheriff go off without me."

"Hey, now," Daniels broke in, rising from the booth. "I think this needs a bit more discussion before we decide. Clay, you've been a good leader. But you have to understand, you haven't been doing this alone. Not by a long shot."

"I know," Clay said. "I'm not saying it's going to be easy. Especially without you guys."

"Then let us come," Daniels said, pounding his fist on the table. The plates and knives shook, clattering against one another.

The wind gusted outside, a reminder that the weather was a constant factor. From where he sat, Clay could see some of the blood spatter from Ralph's suicide.

"I can't do that," Clay said. "And there's no time for arguments. Literally every second that ticks by, my daughter is out there alone. Needing me." He shook his head.

"Daniels, I suggest you be ready to go tomorrow morning. There will be no further discussion. Our separate teams leave at first light."

18.

C lay woke before the others the next morning; fitful dreams prevented him from getting a full night's rest. Despite the lack of sleep, he again felt fierce, his muscles strong and veiny from the work of the nanites. His mind was constantly rolling, making contingency plans.

This was the end of an era. He felt like he'd been leading these people for years.

He walked to the diner as the rest of the crew packed necessities. Items that resembled a rough camping excursion rather than normal travel items of more modern time. Once in the kitchen, he fixed a large stack of toast and put it next to the last of the peanut butter and jam on an old-fashioned serving cart. He found a small flask in the drawer. He sniffed the liquid then sipped it, allowing the whiskey to flow over his tongue. It had been a long time since he'd had a drink—not since Carterville. But now, it turned his stomach, twisted his mind. He needed to stay alert, sharp. He threw the flask into a cabinet.

He pushed the cart back to the others, and watched them eat silently with their packs at their feet. Brandon hadn't said a word since the previous day.

Alayna appeared beside him. She'd braided her

hair, exposing her bright, tanned face. She dropped her pack and grabbed the peanut butter. "Strange, eating something so ordinary on such a weird day."

The others nodded silently. Jacobs and Marcia ate the last of their toast and returned to their neutralizer, packing it with bubble wrap and blankets, making sure it didn't get knocked around on their journey. The other one was already packed and tucked close to Lane's things. Lane's face gave away no emotion. Perhaps she was too practical for it.

Above all, Clay sensed that they were centered on a singular goal, perhaps for the first time since they'd left Carterville. This was the way forward, their only option.

They left the plates, not bothering to wash up. Lane had stretched body bags over the two crazed in the laboratory, knowing they didn't have time to give them a proper burial. A few fingers dangled below one of the covers, like alien appendages.

They stepped out one by one into the sunlight. Maybe because the world was indifferent to their emotions, the sun seemed friendly and beaming. They lined up with Clay in the lead, his head bowed. He felt like a pastor on the last day of church.

"Thank you for following me here," he said, his words somber. He looked each of them in the eye. "I want to remind you that the reason we're still alive is because we have hope. And I want you to hold onto that, no matter which direction you're going today."

His words hung in the air. Daniels stepped forward and wrapped his arms around Clay, patting him on the back with incredible strength, making Clay's back sting. He didn't cry, he didn't speak. He gave Alayna a tentative wave, alluding to those days when he'd flirted with her to the point of exhaustion—once telling her she should be so lucky to receive him.

Those were days long gone.

But Alayna hugged him anyway, tears in her eyes. There wasn't time for hard feelings. Everyone knew that now.

Daniels gestured to the others, who, one by one, hugged Alayna, Clay, and Lane, before mounting their mopeds. Brandon held onto Clay for an extra moment, his thin arms childlike.

"You're going to be okay, kid," Clay said, borrowing Ralph's nickname for the boy. "Just trust me on this one. You're so much stronger than you even know."

Clay, Lane, and Alayna stood in the middle of the empty street, watching the others roar away toward Earlton. As they dwindled into the distance, Clay feared for their safety. They were out of his purview now. And he didn't know if he'd ever learn their fate.

Alayna touched his arm, grounding him in their ever-changing reality. Her dark eyes seemed to bore into his soul. "It's going to be okay, Clay," she said, sounding almost motherly. "We have our path, and they have theirs. As you said. Sticking together would not only be dangerous, it would be a waste of time."

Clay nodded. He heard Lane whisk her keys from her pocket, jangling them in the air. "Let's get this show on the road," she said, her voice light in contrast to the somberness of the difficult farewell.

The three of them walked around the corner from the candy shop, where the scientist's Jeep was parked. It was orange, sturdy, confident. The very vehicle for this post-apocalyptic world. As Clay reached for the driver's door handle, Lane cut in front of him.

"No one drives my car," she said firmly. "Not even you, fearless leader."

Clay laughed, grabbing her supplies and organizing them in the back. He popped into the passenger seat, watching Alayna ease into the back. This was forward motion. This was one step closer to his daughter.

This was the open road.

19.

Twenty minutes outside of Helen, Clay twisted the radio knob, searching for a signal.

"You really think you'll find something out there?" Alayna asked, half-laughing. "It's not like radio will go on when the world ends."

"Maybe somebody's out there, broadcasting what's going on." Clay shrugged.

He turned the knob a bit further, landing on an oldies station that seemed to be playing tapes from a few years before. "Today is September 25, 2014, and we've got the oldies for you," the DJ said in a zippy voice. "Here's Paul Anka."

Alayna groaned in the back seat, tossing her head back. She was surrounded by supplies, with several sacks on her lap, and her face was strained. "This is what my mother used to listen to," she grumbled.

"Well, this is all we have," Clay said. "And I, for one, would rather listen to music than the thoughts in my own head."

"Agreed," Lane said. "But we can turn it down just a little bit. I feel like Paul Anka's trying to wake the dead."

Alayna snickered, not unkindly, and Clay reduced the volume. Lane drove swiftly down the abandoned highway, gorgeous scenery on all sides. The sun crept close to the brown and green flecked mountains.

"You never really see it when you live here," Clay observed. "You don't notice the beauty. I wish I could see it all the time."

"All the more terrifying, thinking of these mountains as places for the crazed to hide out in," Lane murmured. "Perfect little canyons for them. We don't yet know if they can breed. But they certainly learn from one another. And they don't die of natural causes."

"That gives me the creeps," Alayna said. "Maybe turn up Paul Anka again."

"Ha," Lane said, gripping the steering wheel with tight fingers. "Anyway, Clay. I haven't asked you for a few days. How are you feeling since our last round of tests?"

"Physically, I feel amazing," Clay said. "Stronger than ever. I should start measuring my muscles to see how much they grow over a week's time. I can feel them filling out."

"You do look amazing," Alayna said from the back. After a pause, she corrected herself. "I mean, when you had your shirt off the other day, I could see, um, the definition . . ."

Clay didn't speak. Neither did Lane. The sudden, slight, sexual energy sparked in the air between Clay and Alayna, making it difficult for Clay to breathe. An image of her bouncing breasts above him as they made love went through his mind. He gulped.

"Oh shit," Lane said. They had crested a hill, revealing a scattering of abandoned cars in front of them. She slowed to a crawl, taking her time to weave through them, driving from shoulder to median.

"They just left them out here. Do you think they were attacked?"

"Maybe someone in their car turned while they were driving," Alayna said softly. "What would you do if you were trying to get your family to safety, and then someone in the car suddenly became what you were running from?"

"Jesus," Lane said. "Hard to think about."

"Where's your family, Lane?" Clay asked in an attempt to lighten the mood. "Have you been able to contact them?"

"They live in England, actually," Lane replied. "I'm an only child, and my dad's been a professor over there for about ten years now. They up and moved. Tired of American politics."

"And you haven't talked to them since the outbreak?" Clay said.

Lane shook her head, her eyebrows lowering as she came up on another batch of cars. "Marcia and I have been cut off from communication, and we've hardly thought past the epidemic. Our radio signal couldn't reach beyond Helen, and it wasn't connecting with the military base. So I didn't even try my parents, knowing I would probably be disappointed."

No one spoke, recognizing that this kind of talk would just make them feel more desolate.

Clay turned up the oldies channel, allowing the crooning of Frank Sinatra to fill their ears like cotton balls. The day was just beginning.

20.

Lane continued to drive swiftly down the road, encountering the occasional cluster of vehicles. They didn't speak for nearly an hour, each of them lost in their own thoughts. The cars they saw were empty. Clay peeked into their windows as they passed, catching sight of the occasional abandoned purse, or an empty snack wrapper. He imagined the families that belonged to these vehicles. With a jolt, he spotted a car seat in the back of a bright red car, a reminder that young children were a part of this horrible reality too.

In the next five miles, they came upon twelve cars, all slanted in various directions, and even going into the median. Lane stopped short, smacking her hands against the steering wheel. "Well, shit," she said. "I don't know how I'm going to get around this."

Clay leaned forward, eyeing the tight gaps between the cars. "How weird. So many of them stopping at once. It's hard to imagine what happened."

He turned down the radio and Lane veered off to the right taking the Jeep off the shoulder. The tires rolled into the dust and grass, spitting rocks onto the pavement. With a sudden lurch, Alayna was jarred into the window. She moaned loudly, but the others were too focused on the off-roading ahead to notice.

The Jeep bounced side to side as they navigated the ditch. The tires barreled over a bit of debris, making a loud crunching noise. Lane cried out in surprise. "Shit. I'm sorry!" she said, coming to a halt. "What was that? Jesus, that was loud."

"We have to keep moving," Clay said to her. "If we stop, we won't have the momentum to climb out of the ditch. It won't matter what we hit."

Lane set her jaw and stepped on the gas pedal, driving recklessly through the dried grass. With a final jolt, the wheels squealed and spun, and then pushed them back onto the pavement. She sighed with relief, turning her eyes toward the horizon.

"Wow. A bit of excitement," Alayna joked, rubbing her cheek, which was beginning to bruise.

"I'm pretty inexperienced at off-roading," Lane admitted. Her shoulders relaxed slightly. "You know, I haven't seen a single sign of life since we started. Just desolation. And the empty cars."

She picked up speed. Clay looked back, watching the sunlight glinting off the cars. "So, what are your thoughts about why these clusters keep happening?" he asked.

"Surely they just all break down at the same time," Alayna said sarcastically, rolling her eyes. "Everyone forgot to fill up at the gas station, at the same time. Isn't that always it?"

"Ha," Clay said. "If only. What do you think, Lane?"

Lane pressed her lips together tightly, looking pensive. "I'm not sure I want to imagine," she said.

Silence.

Clay leaned his head back. He was getting hungry. With the nanites strengthening his muscles, he seemed to require more food than normal. He closed his eyes, imagining he was driving home to Valerie's cooking. What a blessing that had been. He hadn't known to be thankful for it.

"I do have a theory." Alayna said, breaking the silence. "I think the first car was the problematic one. Especially back there. It was a shitty car, a late 90s model. How do you expect something like that to take you so far out of town?"

"So it starts with the first car?" Clay asked, assessing her theory. "And then what?"

"The second one probably stops to check in on the first one," she continued, speaking as if she were telling Clay about a perp—just like old times. "The second one begins speaking to the first one. Light chitchat, maybe. Talking about what they're going to do. And, especially, talking about how ridiculous this apocalypse is. Ha." A small wrinkle appeared between her eyebrows. "And then something horrible happens. Say, a pack of crazed attack. The second driver doesn't have time to get back to his car. The third and fourth and fifth cars don't recognize initially what the situation is. But soon enough, the first few drivers become crazed themselves. And it continues, like some kind of fucked up string of horror that feeds itself."

"Shit," Lane murmured. "I told you I didn't want to think about it."

"You haven't been out here long enough," Alayna said. "You were safe inside your lab. You'll need to think about it soon. This shit haunts you after a while. Doesn't it, Clay?"

As Clay searched for an answer that wouldn't terrify Lane, they heard a bang beneath them. Lane shrieked as the Jeep began to swerve, pulling them off to the side of the roadway. She slammed on the brakes. Alayna was thrown forward, and struck her head against the top of the Jeep.

After several reckless measures, they skidded to a stop. The trio sat gasping, sweat pouring down their foreheads. The Jeep sat, skewed on the road, almost in the median. It was clear: a tire had blown out.

"Oh God," Lane gasped. "Oh my God, what are we going to do?"

"Calm down!" Clay said. "It was probably damaged from the ditch a few miles back. The Jeep has a spare, doesn't it?"

Lane nodded. She let go of the steering wheel, deep marks in her palms where she'd clung to it too tightly. She wiped her sweating hands on her jeans and jumped out, walking to the back and out of sight.

"You okay, Alayna?" Clay asked. "I heard your head hit—"

"Yeah, sure," Alayna said, blinking several times. "Jesus, it hurt. But I'll be fine. I just hope we get back on the road soon. It's nerve-racking, being out here in the middle of nowhere. It felt much safer when there were six of us. More protection."

"We'll get there faster this way," Clay said firmly. He climbed out and walked to the back, where Lane was pounding her fist on the spare tire. Her face looked almost skeletal. Clay's heart dropped.

"It's useless, isn't it?" he said, already recognizing it. "Jesus."

"It's not damaged," Lane said, clinging to the tire. "It's just flat."

"Well, that doesn't help much, does it?" Alayna said, joining them.

"I can't believe I didn't check it before we left,"

Clay said, leaning heavily against the vehicle. He ran his fingers through his thin hair, wanting to scream.

A sense of dread filled the space around them. Lane flopped the spare on the ground and sat cross-legged on the shoulder, looking out at the horizon. It was clear she felt guilty.

"All right," Clay said, cutting through the silence. "Let's think about this logically. We've been on the road for hours. How far do you think we are from Dearing?"

Lane scratched her eyebrow with a finger. "I think we're probably three or four hours drive away."

"Shit." Alayna turned toward the median. She stood with her arms stretched out, as if she were looking to hitchhike somewhere. Anywhere.

"That's over a day away walking." Clay joined Alayna. Lane was stretched out on the ground, crying.

He hadn't prepared for every possible scenario. And that was his one job, as sheriff—as their de facto leader. Now his daughter was going to pay the price. He, Alayna, and Lane might have to pay, as well.

21.

C lay leaned against the Jeep, staring off into the either. In the distance, fields of long since abandoned rye were verdant, indifferent to the ongoing apocalypse. Between the fields and the highway, steel rails paralleled the road in either direction. A rail car had been left there long enough that it was in a state of decay.

His mind raced. Beside him on the ground, Lane held her hands against her cheeks.

"Clay. I'm so, so sorry," she said remorsefully. "It's my fault. I should have made sure that everything with the Jeep was ready to go. I know I said that nobody drove my car but me. Jesus, you should have been the one driving the entire time."

"Don't beat yourself up too much, Lane," Clay said, leaning down, putting his hands over hers. He pulled them away from her face and peered into her dark eyes. He wanted to insist she be all right, but he knew he couldn't change her feelings. "It's my fault, all right?" he said. "I didn't think about every possibility. And that's on me."

Alayna appeared behind him, casting a shadow across his back. The sun was almost overhead, growing hotter with each passing minute. "What do we do now, Clay? Walk the rest of the way?"

Clay sighed. "That's one option," he said. "We take as many of our supplies as possible, and maybe sleep somewhere halfway, provided we find shelter."

"Jesus," Lane murmured, feeling the weight of his words. "I don't know if I can walk that far."

"It's a good point, Clay. She hasn't been out here with us for very long," Alayna said. "What about back in the last cluster of cars? I think I saw another Jeep. Maybe it'll have a spare we can use."

Clay had seen it too, but hadn't given it a second thought. And now, it was their potential solution.

"That's a possibility." He stood and reached for Lane. She grabbed his hand and pulled herself up. "If it's not damaged or flat."

"Don't we have to take that chance?" Alayna said.

Clay didn't answer right away. He imagined walking back to the cluster of cars and finding nothing, just an empty hole without a spare. They'd have to walk all the way back, wasting the rest of the day and growing more fatigued with every step.

"I should just go myself," Clay said thoughtfully. "I can walk back and check it out. Grab the spare if it's good, and bring it back. I could be back here in two hours, tops. I've got this nanite power in me," he said, trying to make a joke. "I might as well use it."

Lane's eyes were wide and panicked, Alayna still clung to her bad-ass persona.

"You girls okay waiting here?" Clay asked. "Or should we go together?"

Alayna tipped her head at Lane, leaving the decision up to her. Lane checked her watch with then said softly, "There's no point in all of us going. If you think you can get back here in a few hours, then you best get on it. It's getting hot as hell."

Clay scratched the back of his neck and stared down the road in the direction of the other cars. He realized then that he hadn't been alone, without other survivors, since this all started. Not having anyone to watch out for made him edgy, as if he didn't really matter unless he was holding up his friends.

Jesus. Being a sheriff was engrained in him more than he'd realized.

"All right," Clay said. He grabbed his canteen from the back of the Jeep, which still sloshed with water. He slung a rifle over his shoulder, and then snagged the car jack from the tool compartment. He shoved it deep in his backpack, alongside a single granola bar. He zipped it with a quick motion. The sound was familiar, reminiscent of Maia getting ready for school.

"I'll be back as fast as I can," he said, his eyes tracing his companion's faces. He wanted to memorize them. They could be the last faces he ever saw. "Wish me luck."

22.

C lay felt the sway of the rifle against his back as he walked. He'd been walking for over a half hour, and the sweat beads were rolling down his back and his chest. He ripped his shirt from his back and hung it around his neck, blinking up at the bright blue sky. He'd never seen it so open.

He wondered if Maia could see the sky where she was. She'd love it, despite her current "teenage angst" phase. When had that started, anyway? He could see right through it, always. It was a façade. It was, perhaps, the armor she had to wear to survive high school. He couldn't blame her for that. He'd worn similar armor. Hell, he was wearing armor now, protecting himself from the conflicting feelings he had for Alayna. He'd felt miserable ever since he'd slept with her, on the eve of the end of the world. Now, with even a glimmer of hope of surviving, he knew he should be thinking about Valerie instead and protecting himself from pain by doing all he could to keep moving, to keep fighting.

Everyone was just doing what they could to survive.

With Maia constantly on his mind, Clay wondered if she was thinking about him, too. Surely she expected him to come save her. That's what he did, after all. He'd made that very clear from the beginning. And he'd expected many more years of that. Rescuing her from prom, if she had a bad date. Visiting her at college and taking her out for ice cream—or beers, even—and listening to her problems about classes and professors and roommates. He'd take care of it, if only because he listened, and listened well.

He'd made a point to be there for her since she was young. Even more than Valerie, he was the protector. The one Maia had raced to when things went bump in the night.

He couldn't believe that had been an actual time of his life. It had been so fleeting.

When Maia was a little girl, he'd taken her to the playground after work quite often, giving Valerie some time to go to the gym or the grocery store or out for drinks with a few of her girlfriends. He and Maia's time together had become sacred, something of a ritual. He'd pick her up from school and help her load up her backpack, hand her a snack as she chatted cheerfully about what they'd done that day. He could clearly see the image of her biting into a bright green apple, her eyes dancing as she told him about playing the recorder for the first time.

"It was loud and stupid," she'd said.

He hadn't been a musician, either.

At the park one day, Maia had raced off with several of the other children, leaving Clay off to the side, still dressed in his Sherriff's uniform. She'd been seven years old, and he'd trusted her, but still monitored the perimeter. He sat beside one of the mothers, who was reading a magazine about celebrity gossip and didn't bother to look up.

After several minutes without seeing Maia, Clay

had sprung to his feet, feeling terror building in his stomach. He had a sixth sense for things like this— for knowing when his daughter was injured, or frightened. He dashed through the playground hunting for her, past the ruby red slide and around the swings. All of the children were pink-cheeked and pudgy, so unlike his bright, thin-limbed daughter.

"MAIA?" he'd cried, looking behind trees. "MAIA. WHERE ARE YOU?"

The other parents had begun to pay attention, standing up and watching the frantic man in uniform cross through the sandbox. "MAIA!"

Finally, he'd raced to the nearby parking lot, seeing a circle of children gawking down at the ground. Clay had felt his stomach in his throat, bile forming along his tongue. He'd pushed through the crowd to discover his daughter, slim little Maia, with her arm badly broken She looked up at him with the same bright eyes she'd revealed as a tiny newborn, just as frightened, just as shocked.

"Jesus, Maia," he'd said. He'd dialed the ambulance immediately, using his ancient flip phone, and then bent down, careful not to move her. "What happened?"

"I ran after the Frisbee," Maia whimpered, glancing at one of the boys in front of her—probably the onc who threw it. "I'm sorry, Daddy. I know you said to stay where you could see me."

This had stabbed Clay, making him close his eyes momentarily. He could feel Maia's pain palpitating up and down his arm.

He'd righted himself, and brushed down Maia's messy bangs. "Honey, taking risks is a beautiful thing. It's the reason we're alive," he'd told her. "We're alive by chance. And so we have to take those chances, every day."

"But what if we break our arms?" she'd whispered, almost losing consciousness from the pain.

"Then we let them heal, and then we get back out there," Clay had said, as the ambulance stopped nearby. The men had lifted Maia onto a gurney, careful not to jostle her arm.

God, what a memory. Clay had thought that would be the worst thing that ever happened in in his life, feeling responsible for his daughter's well being, even as she was pushing herself to be the best possible, most exciting person she could be.

Clay finally saw the battered Jeep. It was facing him, almost challenging him. The area was eerie, quiet, the other cars ominous. Clay couldn't look at them now, without seeing the scene that Alayna had painted before. It was clear that people had died there.

On closer inspection, the Jeep didn't have a spare. But its tires were in great condition, two of them nearly brand new. With a practiced hand, Clay knelt down and cranked the back of the Jeep high, removing the tire with ease. The sweat that had been pouring down his back was now dried, his skin cool. His muscles seemed to brim with strength and agility, enhanced by the technology. He hoisted the tire onto his bare shoulder, snagging the granola bar from his pack and ripping at the chocolaty snack. The sugar was an instant punch to his brain, the way he'd imagined cocaine to be. He closed his eyes with pleasure.

Should he have tried cocaine? Should he have taken more risks? What was this life now, in comparison? There were no rules. Only those of physics, of biology. And with the nanites rearranging his insides, how could he know how much time he had left?

He turned to go, with his backpack zipped and the tire positioned easily on his shoulder. He had another hour before he got back to the girls and they could continue on toward Dearing. If he could hurry, even just a little, they would reach Maia that much quicker.

A feeling began to spin deep in his gut. And he didn't like it.

He heard a horrendous screech in the distance, somewhere behind him. Every cell, every hair, every muscle tensed. He knew the sound. That sound meant he might never see his daughter again. It meant that safety was only an illusion he'd created in his mind.

That sound meant that the crazed were close. And they were hunting for him.

23.

Frozen in place, Clay sensed that one of the crazed was bounding toward him, perhaps as close as the other vehicles now. He spun to see what was behind him.

The mutant that approached had once been a six-foot tall man, a near-match to Clay himself, with broad shoulders, a thick-ish belly—one surely bred and born from meal after meal from his wife, wherever she lay. It seethed, its eyes wild, bugging out. It strode toward him, it's gate elongated. As it approached it reached out its arms, ready to tear at Clay's throat.

Clay's weapon was over his shoulder, blocked by the tire he was holding. With a surge of energy, he threw the spare tire at it, on instinct more than anything else. Clay was surprised to see the tire sail through the air more than a dozen yards.

"Jesus," he whispered, his jaw dropping. His muscles revved from the pure bliss of the effort, as if they'd craved releasing that kind of power.

The tire blasted directly in the center of its chest, knocking it backward several yards. The impact cracked the monster's ribs, a bone-chilling sound echoing through the air.

It lay on its back for several seconds, but Clay

remained alert, watching. Huffing, it pushed the tire off his chest and started to hum a sort of guttural chant, which swelled into a low, horrible growl. It drew chills along Clay's neck and arms, but he remained still, watching, waiting.

Then in the distance—at the crest of the hill—four more of the crazed appeared. Cracking his neck first to the right, then to the left, Clay focused on the approaching monsters. The first one had let loose a grating battle cry, apparently alerting others of their impending attack.

He pulled his rifle from his shoulder, raising it in a smooth motion. The nearest crazed effortlessly flung the tire to the side before rising to its feet. Blood and entrails oozed from its chest, looking like the remains of some mad experiment dripping down its half-torn shirt. Clay couldn't remember the last time he'd felt disgusted—something that made him turn away.

You could get used to anything, he guessed.

As it approached, Clay fired a bullet through its head. It collapsed, dust puffing up from the road.

But the others were approaching rapidly, forcing Clay to turn his attention to them, energized, alert. He aimed at the far left one.

"Today's the day, fucker," he whispered.

When the crazed monster was ten or so feet away, Clay fired a bullet into its brain, then into the brains of the rest, leaving a pile of bodies.

Clay's gunshots echoed out over the mountains, making his ears ring. The guttural screaming told him that more crazed were coming, wanting a piece of the action.

Leaping to action himself, Clay grabbed the tire from the side of the road, seeing the blood of the crazed dripping from the rubber to the ground. Heaving it over his shoulder once again, he turned and began his trek back toward his stranded companions. He knew they were losing time—and quite possibly losing humanity. He started to run, feeling no sense of exhaustion. And being alone with his thoughts left him with considerable self-doubt. It wasn't ideal for his sense of survival—his sense of purpose.

If everyone was dead, why should he go on? he thought. His tongue had its own heartbeat, a reminder that he needed water, he needed more oxygen, he needed food to remain alive.

But it was all for Maia, his brain whispered back. For Maia. This became his mantra as he drove forward, his feet pounding against the pavement, his toes bleeding, the nails digging into the skin.

If he was going to keep fighting, it would have to be for her. It couldn't be for anyone else. And certainly not for himself.

24.

It was nearly forty minutes later when Clay returned to where he'd left Lane and Alayna, what felt like a million years before. Coughing slightly, his throat raspy, he realized that he was standing in the precise place they'd broken down—he could even see the ragged, black tire marks and the abandoned railway car. This was certainly the place.

But the Jeep—and the women—were nowhere in sight.

His heart ramping up, he dropped the tire to the ground, scanning the horizon. "Fuck. Fuck," he bellowed. His skin tingled and grew cold as his mind raced. Several scenarios played out in his thoughts, including one involving the women just pretending that the Jeep was broken down, calculating a way to leave him behind.

Maybe they feared for their lives, maybe he was showing increased signs of being crazed, too crazy to be around other humans. He was growing increasingly stronger, practically inhuman. Maybe when you turned, you didn't recognize it in yourself until it was too late, until suddenly you were eating another's flesh, tasting the juicy blood and allowing it to roll down your tongue.

"Fuck," he grumbled.

Of course, there were other options. The women could have been taken, kidnapped by some deranged individual. Or something much more horrifying. They could have been eaten by the crazed. He had no real understanding of the world outside of Carterville, and knew that humans were animals, first and foremost, and would ultimately form packs, protecting themselves from outsiders.

Dropping to his knees, Clay tried to breathe, panting loudly at the ground, biting his lip with worry. Tangy blood coated his mouth, making him swallow clumsily, trying to get the taste out. A spark of anger ignited. He was completely alone—without food or extra ammunition—without his companions. And, most of all, without the device that could end this horrible war.

Looking down at his rifle, his mind presented an alternative: suicide. Perhaps his only option.

"No. Fuck that," Clay said, ramming his fists against the pavement. "I have to find Maia. I can't let this stop me."

He heard a grinding from the far side of the road. Lifting his head, Clay watched as the door of the abandoned railway car creaked open, revealing a dark head of hair, an eager-looking face. A hesitant smile.

It was Alayna, perhaps his only friend left in the world.

"Jesus!"

"Get over here!" she called, waving her arm. "And hurry!"

Leaving the tire in the road, Clay raced to the railcar, hoping the image of Alayna wouldn't fade away like a mirage.

When he reached it, Alayna wrapped her arms

around him, hugging him close. She was trembling.

"Quickly," she whispered into his ear. "Come inside."

Clay leaped into the shadowy car and Lane pushed the door closed, using muscle he hadn't known she had. She turned toward Clay, her hands against her chest, as if in prayer.

"What's going on?" Clay asked, his voice echoing. He didn't want to tell them he'd thought they were dead—or worse, that they'd abandoned him on purpose.

"It was horrible," Lane breathed, blinking rapidly. "It happened so fast."

Clay turned to Alayna, recognizing her as the voice of reason. "What do you mean?"

"A big caravan of off-road trucks approached us just after you left," Alayna said. She swiped her hair behind her ears, trying to uphold a standard of reporting—just as if this was a normal day back at the station. "We didn't want to stick around to find out their intentions. Despite my police training, in this world, two women left alone and stranded on the side of the road isn't the best scenario. If you catch my drift."

"I do," Clay murmured, not wanting to say he'd already thought of it. "I'm glad you hid. It was a smart move."

Alayna grimaced, a sign of hesitation that Clay couldn't put his finger on.

"And the Jeep?" Clay asked.

"Their leader checked out the Jeep. We heard him say that the engine was still warm. He ordered that they change the tire from one of the other vehicles. Apparently, it was in better shape than some of theirs. They had it fixed in less than ten minutes. Something that was holding us up for hours. And for them—" she trailed off.

"We left the keys in the ignition," Lane finished, her eyes toward the ground. "It was a mistake. We just panicked."

"That's the worst of it," Alayna affirmed. "If we'd only thought to grab the fucking keys—"

Clay exhaled sharply, not wanting to reprimand the girls. What on Earth would he say, anyway? No form of "you should have done" would fix their current problem. He'd gone all the way back, nearly been eaten by five crazed monsters, all for nothing.

"Which direction did they go?" he asked.

"There's a side road we didn't see out there," Alayna said. "A dirt one. They went that way, out of sight. And we've been in here ever since, just praying you'd come back." Alayna touched his hands, tracing a line down his bloodied fingers. "And you did," she whispered, her voice tired.

Clay allowed it, although he wanted to pull his hand away. He was shaking.

"And the supplies?" he asked, his anxiety growing.

Alayna pulled her hand away.

"All the food—and ammunition—was inside the Jeep," Lane stammered. "We didn't even think of it. Didn't have the chance to grab it."

"Jesus," Clay murmured, bowing his head. He blinked. "And the device. That's gone too. Our only fucking hope."

Before either of the girls could answer, he heard a shuffle. Lane ripped open her backpack, revealing the device within. It glinted in the light slicing in from a crack in one of the side walls. Clay nodded his head in relief.

"Good. All isn't lost, after all."

Silence settled in and Clay knew he needed to make the effort to change his mood—keep the morale high.

"Just no food or water," Lane said. "And if we're going to make it to Dearing, we're going to have to find a way to stay hydrated."

"We still have several hours of daylight left," Clay said, eyeing his watch. His mind revved. "If we leave right now, we can get halfway to Dearing. Maybe we can find a river or a creek on the way. Possibly find something to eat."

"We're so, so sorry, Clay," Alayna whispered.

"Don't mention it," Clay said firmly. "But there's no use sitting here and waiting. We've got to get a move on."

25.

C lay yanked the door of the rail car back, revealing the intense sunlight. He pushed toward the road, and began to walk the path toward Dearing. Alayna and Lane made a kind of triangle formation behind him. Their walk was monotonous. Their mouths held no words. Shadows drew out behind them, growing longer with the passing of time—something Clay no longer felt, at least, not in the old way—the clock ticked away. The sun rose and set, but the hours were different now.

His mind had returned to thoughts of Maia and Valerie. Time had felt strange when Maia had gone to the hospital for that broken arm, sure—but it had felt even worse when Valerie had had the cancer scare a few years later, when Maia was ten. They'd taken her in for a routine scan and then asked her to remain overnight for additional tests. Poised on the back porch, waiting for the call with Maia seated beside him, sipping an over-sugared iced tea, Clay had imagined his life without Valerie for the first time. The first time since he'd first kissed her in high school, knowing, once and for all, that they would be together for the rest of their lives.

He hadn't reckoned that the "rest of their lives" could ever be so short.

There, on the back porch, with ten-year-old Maia, he considered it.

How would he know how to raise Maia alone? How would he know what to buy for her? How would he tell her not to wear short skirts, not to run after boys, not to waste her life on her silly high school friends?

How would he explain to her that her mother would have to be buried, deep in the ground, never to be seen again? How would he take Maia to the gravesite, ask her to pick out flowers, to abandon her the life of the living to pray over her dead mother?

How could he do any of it?

He was getting ahead of himself, and he knew it. But deep in the waves of sudden misery, he had nothing to do but think through every possibility, preparing himself for what could occur.

Thankfully, Valerie had called him that night, telling him all was fine; the lump was nothing but a strange collection of ordinary cells, which they would eventually remove in a few years, just in case. Clay had loaded a slumbering Maia into the car, driving swiftly to the hospital to pick up his wife, not allowing her to sleep there alone. He'd forced her to remain awake till two in the morning, as he kissed every inch of her body, never realizing before how fleeting their life together could possibly be.

She'd been exhausted, achy. But she'd seen the desperation in his eyes, and she'd allowed it, giggling before falling into a deep slumber, draped across his chest. None of them had gone anywhere the next day: not to school, to the station. Not to work. They'd allowed themselves the simple pleasure of normalcy.

It had been one of the best days of Clay's life.

"Clay."

Clay blinked rapidly, trying to bring himself back to reality.

"Hey. Clay!" Alayna shouted.

Clay lifted his head, eyeing the horizon. The bright, orange sun was drawing closer to it, making the mountains glow, the trees becoming twiggy shadows.

"Clay, I saw something," Alayna said. She pulled her gun from her shoulder, pointing it toward something in the distance.

Clay swung his arm back, pushing the barrel toward the ground.

"What the hell?" Alayna whispered. "Clay?"

"No shooting," Clay murmured. "Let's use the device."

"Why?" Alayna said. "I can knock him out with a quick shot."

"I know. I know," Clay murmured, his eyes darting about. He hadn't yet caught sight of the monsters. "Before, when I got the tire, I shot at the crazed. But the gunfire echoed off the mountains, drawing others toward me. It was like an announcement a. I don't want to take the risk again."

Lane slipped her backpack from her shoulders, unzipping it with a swift motion and handing him the device. She spoke in a hushed voice.

"You're going to want to be about a dozen meters away when you hit this button," she said pointing to one of two buttons. "It'll charge it up. And then, just pull the trigger. About the same pressure you need to squeeze the trigger of a gun."

"A dozen meters," Clay confirmed.

"I can come with you, if you want," Lane said.

"No. I don't want to take any risks. I need both of you to hide. Immediately."

Alayna pressed her lips together. "You shouldn't have to do this alone."

But he did. Clay pointed at a dried-up irrigation canal where the girls could hide. "Go," he whispered fiercely. "I don't want to ask again."

26.

Clay waited as the girls hustled toward the ditch. Satisfied with their cover, he spun toward the movement ahead and began his pursuit. With each stride forward, his anticipation increased.

It was nearly time.

He was well aware that the same nanites pulsing their way through the crazed monsters' bodies also flourished deep within him. Triggering the device meant potentially ending his own existence. With a single flick of the button, he could be leaving Alayna and Lane to fend for themselves.

He could be abandoning Maia.

Fuck. Fuck. Could he really do it, knowing it could very well mean suicide? Looking down at the device, which flashed ominously in the orange sunset, he felt his mind bend. He felt as if he were about to leap over a deep crevasse, not knowing if the rope would hold fast behind him.

"Here goes nothing," he said.

But he didn't have time to think for long. A crazed monster lurched from behind the trees toward him. Its limbs flailed; blood oozed from its mouth. Its eyes bulged from its face, revealing bright green irises.

"What beautiful eyes you have," Clay said softly,

lifting the device and aiming it at the crazed. Adrenaline pumped in his veins. "Better to see you with, my dear."

The monster neared him, its ripped shirt fluttering in the wind. Bony fingers stretched out, revealing broken, cracked nails, each covered with what was most likely somebody else's blood.

"You fucking bastard," Clay muttered. "Jesus Christ. I hope this works."

As it came into range, Clay pressed the primary button, held his breath, and then squeezed the trigger. He closed his eyes in sudden panic.

But nothing happened.

Clay kept his finger on the trigger, still squeezing, as if it would blow a projectile from its non-existent barrel. Or reveal in some other way that it was activated—that it was working.

Still, nothing happened. The crazed was approaching rapidly, its greedy fingers reaching for its next victim.

"No—" Clay could hear the wail in his voice. If this didn't work, all of humanity would fall to these creatures. There'd be no purpose, no reason to move forward. "Fuck you—you fucking bastard—"

The crazed's footsteps began to falter, as if it was running on fumes. Its eyes suddenly fixed, its arms flailed without reason before dropping to its waist. Blinking at Clay, it appeared to see the sheriff for the first time—with near-human eyes. Then, its stare was vacant again, like a dead person, staring from the beyond.

Jesus.

It dropped onto its knees and fell forward, smashing its nose against the pavement. An odd colored blood oozed out, puddling on the ground.

Clay stared at the monster, shocked, with his finger still on the trigger.

But nothing else came. No shots had been fired. Nothing echoed against the walls of the surrounding canyons, revealing their location. He'd done it, and he'd survived. And he'd killed one of the crazed in an apparently non-violent way.

"Shit," Clay said blankly, finally removing his finger from the trigger and examining the neutralizer, recognizing, but not understanding its considerable power. He whistled quietly. His heart pounded against his ribcage. He was still alive.

For a moment, he forgot everything. He forgot his wife, his daughter. He forgot the rest of the world, spinning on a benign axis. With this, he was invincible.

Alayna and Lane scampered from the irrigation canal moments later. They looked on, awed, as Clay continued to stare at his victim. Alayna reached out, pressing her palm against his lower back.

"You okay there, Sheriff?" she asked, her voice shallow.

Clay didn't move. Alayna took a step forward, aligning herself beside him. Lane did the same on his other side, forming a kind of wall. They stared at the first to die as a result of the device. It felt almost like church, this prayer-like formation over the bleeding body. In the distance, the sun began to dip below the horizon, assuring them that night was falling. Life would continue . . . for the moment.

"Well," Clay said finally. "I'm still here."

"You are," Lane said.

"And that's at least something," he said

Alayna just smiled. Her arms dangled, as if she was at a complete loss, not knowing how to hold her body, her head, her face.

Clay passed the neutralizer back to Lane, letting it go regretfully. "It worked like a charm, Lane," he said, his composure returning to normal. "I'm impressed. I never gave much thought to you science types. But this . . . was . . . quite impressive."

He gave her a half-smile, teasing her.

"Your backhanded compliment is graciously accepted," Lane said, attempting a laugh. They hadn't been able to laugh in a long time. It was a tired gasp, and wouldn't have sounded happy in any other context. But here, it sounded like hope.

Clay looked at his watch. "It's going to get dark soon," he said. "I think we should start looking for a place to crash for the night."

"So many options," Lane said, almost sarcastic, pointing toward the canyons—a world they would most likely never have faced in their previous lives.

"I think we should get off the road," Clay said. "Find something with higher terrain, maybe."

To the right, a trail snaked off from the main road, tracing up and into the hills.

"Even if we can't find a building, there are more trees up there. More places to hide. Maybe we'll even find a few rabbits or squirrels to eat."

Alayna scrunched up her nose, saying nothing. Lane zipped the device back in her bag and slid it over her shoulder.

"Strange he was alone," Alayna said, gesturing a final time toward the dead crazed on the road. "Normally they're in packs."

"Maybe not. Maybe the sound of the attack draws more of them in," Clay said. "But your guess is as good as mine. I'm just glad that it's over for now."

"I swear. If I walk another mile, my bones will break," Lane moaned. "You might have to carry me up that hill."

Clay moved toward the trail, sensing that his bones and muscles were in far better condition than Lane's, even without food and water. It was as if he'd been rehabbing for years, as if he'd been fueling with near-constant protein. He was energized, ready to run a marathon. He'd never wanted to run in his life. Even the gut, once a topic of teasing from Valerie, had melted away, revealing well defined abs.

"Come on, gang. We can rest at the top of the hill," Clay said. "Just gotta keep moving. As much as we can."

27.

T hey hiked up the cliffside trail, Alayna and Lane
leading, with Clay bringing up the rear. The
girls' steps were uneven, scattering rocks beneath
them and nearly blasting Clay in the face a few times.
Each time, they regained their composure, their
balance, their own faces scrunching with fear.

"Imagine if we fell all the way down," Alayna said,
glancing toward the snaking road far below. "All this
fighting—surviving. And for what? To be broken—
and quite possibly dead, lying at the bottom of some
stupid cliff."

"I thought about that so often when I played that
game as a kid. Oregon Trail," Lane said. "How they'd
made this huge, life-changing decision to trek across
the entire country. To change their lives. To strike it
rich. Whatever. And so often, you died from cholera
or dysentery or starvation . . . in a place just like
around here, in Colorado," she said, half-laughing.
"First off, good for us for landing in a place that used
to kill thousands of people a year. Does that make us
hardier than the rest of the country? Or just more
foolish?"

"At this point, mankind seems like the most
foolish experiment I've ever encountered," Alayna
said, chortling for the first time in a while. "Only a

few months ago, I was worried that I wasn't going to recover from a silly fight with my on-again, off-again girlfriend. And now, I'm worried I won't survive the night. Life really flips over on you."

"We're just a part of someone else's experiment. Someone else's computer game," Lane said, grasping at limbs and twigs along the trail for support. "Just pixels."

Clay didn't join the conversation. He kept his nose pointed upward, his eyes searching the top of the hill, hunting for good opportunities for shelter. He was worried about rain, knowing that once they got damp and chilly, they'd be susceptible to illness. Finally, something caught his eye. Pointing toward an overgrown area of bushes and tall trees, he said, "Let's check that out."

The girls slowed their tired legs, allowing Clay to step around and lead them off the path and through the weeds. Sweat poured down their faces; dehydration bleeding them dry. Clay glanced back at them and thought they resembled two skeletons, both hunched over, the hollows of their cheeks prominent. Their lips were chapped, specks of dead skin surrounding the darkness of their mouths.

If he didn't get some food and water in them soon, they would all be stuck in the woods, too exhausted to continue.

Once in the stand of trees, Lane and Alayna collapsed in the shadows. Alayna leaned her head against her backpack, whipping her gun from around her shoulders. "Just end me now," she whispered, sounding foolish. "So tired."

Lane eased her cheek to the grass, humming to herself. "It feels as comfortable as any bed," she whispered. "I could sleep like this for days."

"I'm going to go see if I can find some water or food," Clay said, pointing deeper into the forest. "Before it gets too dark. Still light enough that I can see."

"Be careful out there," Alayna said.

"Don't run off again like last time," Clay teased. "You nearly gave me a panic attack."

He turned away, oddly grateful to leave them behind, if just for a little while. He eased through the overgrowth, stopping a few times and dropping low to the ground to listen intently for sounds of wildlife. His arms brimmed with energy as he righted himself effortlessly. Pumping upward, toward the top of the hill, he marveled at the beautiful canyons around him—wondering if he'd ever take a leisurely hike again. Back in the old days, people hadn't hiked for fun. They'd lived, walking from place to place, finding no joy in it. Having to do it out of necessity. Perhaps that was the future, as well.

After nearly a half an hour, Clay heard a stream bubbling in the near distance. Once he reached it, he knelt down, sipping directly from the water and wetting his nose, his hair, his cheeks. The sweat rinsed off and into the stream, cleansing him. He was being rejuvenated, completely and totally.

Without delay, he produced the large canteen from his side, watching as the water filled it. Easing back through the forest, he found the path back without even thinking, as if instinct had taken over. He was now running in pure survival mode.

But his excursion wasn't entirely fruitful. He found no signs of food. No berries. No squirrels. Nothing. He could try again later.

When he got to the women, they were half-delirious, their heads still on the grass. Clay handed

Alayna the canteen, watching as her mouth was drawn to it, like a bee to pollen. She drank greedily, snorting slightly, before passing the canteen to Lane and swiping the back of her hand across her mouth. Her face was still covered in sweat.

"Clay?" she whispered. "I'm so tired."

"I know," Clay said. He remained standing, his fresh face looking bright and eager.

"You look fine," Alayna said softly, perhaps revealing feelings that remained, bubbling beneath the surface. "How do you do it? How do you stay so— so perfect?"

"It's the nanites," Lane said, forcing her mouth away from the canteen. "He's like a top-tier athlete now. Nothing can stop him. Just look at that body. He's even more muscular now than he was when he arrived in Helen."

Clay didn't blush. Lane passed the water back to Alayna. "You girls think that if we get a good night's sleep here, we can move on tomorrow?"

"I can tell you that I'll try my hardest," Alayna said. "That's all I can really give you, Clay."

Lane nodded, her hair swirling around her ears. "Some food would help, I think."

"That's easier said than done right now," Clay said. He found a spot near a tree, a short distance away. Stretching his muscular legs out, he felt them relax after their something like twelve or thirteen miles of walking. "We can try again tomorrow. Just drink as much water as your body can hold and get some sleep."

Alayna looked at him, her eyes shining, almost pleading. But Clay ignored her, aware of her need. He remembered the way she'd traced his finger after he'd killed the crazed with the neutralizer. Did she not understand that he needed to be with his wife, to focus on his daughter? Did she not realize that them being together was a pure mistake, nothing more?

"Sleep. Right," Lane said, snorting slightly. "Trying to sleep at the end of the world is like trying to sleep when you think Santa's on his way. You never really know what you're going to get in the morning. But in this case, I don't think I really want to find out."

"Just relax," Clay murmured. "No use worrying. You're just going to make yourself sick. And then they win."

But he didn't particularly feel as if the crazed would win the war. At least, not now. His body was agile, lithe. He could defeat half an army of crazed, with a single flick of the trigger. Worry dropped away, and he relaxed completely, listening to the ragged breathing of the women across the clearing.

28.

As the minutes ticked into hours, the brutality of night fell around them. What had been a warm day settled into a deep chill. While Clay remained alert—his eyes still staring up at the tops of trees—he knew that the girls were not doing well. He could almost feel their shivers through the grass; he could hear their chattering teeth.

Still, he thought, maybe they'd get some much-needed rest despite the harsh environment. It was like Maia, back home in the crib, crying out for his and Valerie's attention. They'd grown accustomed to racing in to check on her, to ensure she was all right. And each time, it seemed certain that she'd just cried out to them because she was lonely, that she didn't want to let them go. Gradually, they'd had to force themselves to stay away, allowing little Maia to cry it out.

Clay felt no discomfort whatsoever. But after nearly an hour of their continued quivering, he rose and watched as the girls pressed their bodies against one another. Sighing, Clay slipped between them. Immediately, they were drawn like moths to the flame, pressing against him. They continued to shiver, but eventually their breathing slowed. Their eyelids began to droop. Their stress, once a raging beast within each of them, decreased. Lane even found peace and fell asleep, like a child in his arms.

But Alayna remained awake. Clay could sense her mind racing beside him, her lips parting then closing again, her mouth filled with all the things she still wanted to say.

Clay felt it. With Alayna's breasts pressed against his chest, he felt lust welling up, like a massive wave. It crashed over him, and he bit his lip to avoid kissing her. Would they be like this all night, dancing in and out of consciousness, unable to say the things they were feeling?

Did Clay have to explain to her just what he felt? About his wife? About his daughter?

And the lingering worry that if he did sleep with Alayna—which, on so many different levels he really wanted to—he would pass along the nanites. Sure, that would give her superhuman strength and power. It would stop her freezing and her hunger. But it could also destroy her.

He would never do that to her. Not on purpose. Never in a million years.

"Is something wrong?" Alayna finally whispered, her voice raspy.

Clay felt his heart crack down the center. He shook his head, almost imperceptibly. He couldn't form words.

"Ever since we got to Helen," Alayna began, sounding fragile. "You've been so standoffish. Like you don't want to be near me, even—even when I'm the person in your life you know best, right now. I hate to say it, but it's like you don't want to be a part of my life any longer. Clay—I felt things for you. I still feel things for you. I can't deny them—I mean—I still love Megan, of course . . ." She trailed off, her eyes growing wet with tears.

Clay didn't speak. He hated facing reality. He could feel it like a rock in his throat.

Turning his head toward Lane, Clay watched as her chest rose and fell, rose and fell, assuring him she was still asleep. Her eyes danced behind her eyelids, showing her active dreams. At this turning point, in this post-apocalyptic world, Clay could only imagine what her mind created.

"Say something," Alayna begged. "Please. Anything. You're going to destroy me if you don't."

Clay thought for several moments, readjusting on the cold, rock-hard ground. "It's not that I don't think about it," he said finally. "It's just that, if these scientists are telling the truth—if the nanites inside me can really be transmitted virally, then I don't think it's wise that we . . ." He trailed off, leaving the words in the air.

Alayna looked into his eyes, assessing. After a very small forever, she nodded, her chin tucking against his chest. "I see," she whispered. She kissed the warmth at the nape of his neck. Clay's spine tingled. "I think you might be right."

"I knew you'd understand," Clay said. "The reason behind it."

But Alayna pressed on, as if she hadn't heard him. "Just so you know," she said. "If this is the end of the world, the end of life and civilization as we know it, then I don't want to die alone. That's the worst fate of all. Loneliness."

Clay's heart felt squeezed. He wrapped his arm tightly around Alayna, this woman he'd known professionally for years—intimately for far less than that—and stroked her hair, hoping he could comfort her enough to allow her to sleep. Neither of them spoke again. But slowly, surely, he felt Alayna's muscles loosen; he felt her body collapse beside his. Her inhalations came few and far between as she escaped the chilly world around them, finding a very small interval of peace.

29.

Alayna blinked awake the next morning, watching as the sunlight filtered in through the trees above. Shivering slightly, she turned her head toward the warm body beside her, expecting the sturdiness of Clay, his firm embrace. But instead, she was met by the pleasant face of Lane, who was still conked out, her pink lips parted slightly—looking almost sensual.

Alayna had not looked at Lane that way before.

Pulling back slightly, not wanting her to awaken and catch her staring, Alayna traced the outline of Lane's slim form with her eyes, wondering if the she'd ever been with another woman. Alayna had coped with bisexual tendencies since high school, although she'd had to fight for her emotions, for her status in life. Her parents hadn't wanted her to be free with her sexuality, and Carterville had been a small town, full of gossips.

Lane's eyes popped open. She blinked several times at Alayna, as if she were seeing her for the first time. After a long pause, a smile stretched her cheeks.

"Hi," she breathed.

"Hi," Alayna said, giggling slightly, girlishly.

"Where did Clay go?" Lane asked, glancing

around the clearing.

"Who knows?".

"You're saying we don't need him?" Lane asked, her eyes bright, playful. "Because I seem to sense something between the two of you."

"No. That was just a small mistake. Something I don't regret, mind you," Alayna said, rising up on her elbow and bringing her hand to Lane's upper arm. She felt at the firmness of Lane's arm through her shirt.

Lane's left eyebrow nearly leapt from her forehead. "I see," she said.

"In a perfect world, we wouldn't need men. For anything," Alayna said.

"No procreation?"

"Can't we just freeze their sperm for all future generations?"

"Down with men, then?" Lane laughed. "Should we abandon Clay in the wilderness?"

"Could he handle it out here alone?" Alayna asked, laughing.

"You're evil," Lane whispered, leaning toward her. Her lips were mere inches from Alayna's. After craving attention from Clay the night before, Alayna felt her lips tingle with desire. If she just nudged forward, only slightly; if she bridged this distance ...

Clay pushed in through the brush, finding the girls staring at one another, inches apart, their stunning profiles looking almost as if they could fit together, like pieces of a puzzle. He swallowed, then cleared his throat, alerting them that he was there.

Alayna spun toward him, giving him a semi-evil laugh. Was she trying to get back at him for not sleeping with her? Was this one of those games women play, during which they push and pull you, never allowing you to know exactly what they're thinking? He remembered Valerie doing that during her pregnancy, when her hormones had been all out of whack, sending her sobbing into the bedroom some days, breaking plates on others, and then cuddling him till she demanded sex on the good days. The good days never seemed to come often enough.

"Oh. You're here," Lane said, her voice blasé.

"We'd already made peace with the fact that you probably weren't coming back," Alayna said, chuckling. "We'd plotted a future without men."

"It was oddly gorgeous, actually. We'd just freeze a bunch of sperm, recreate civilization without war, without greed—without all that shit you men cause for us. Doesn't it sound like a paradise?" Lane asked, lifting her face away from Alayna's with a swift motion.

Clay laughed nervously, his eyes dancing from Alayna to Lane, then back again. What the hell was going on?

"Well . . . that's nice," he muttered, scratching at the back of his head. Confusion clouded his brain.

"Not just nice," Alayna said. "Life-altering." She winked at Lane, almost cartoonish in her motions. She and Lane burst into laughter, rolling back on the grass and clutching their stomachs. Clay hadn't seen such an uproar since before the crazed had begun their attacks. A smile crept across his face.

"Ha," he blurted. "All right. All right. You've had your fun."

"Oh, we have," Alayna agreed, swiping a tear from her eye. "If only you knew just how much."

Sensing this was a jab, Clay ducked it. "I scouted down the road," he said, trying to steer them back on track. "It's clear as far as the eye can see. I think we're about eight or nine hours away from Dearing. The sooner we get on the road, the better we'll be."

"The better we'll be. You hear that, Alayna? The man has a plan," Lane joked, rising from the grass. "Guess we better listen to him."

Alayna snickered, helping Lane gather their things. They both looked thinner, diminished.

"I refilled the water," Clay said, thrusting the canteen forward. "But still no food."

"Surprise, surprise," Alayna teased him. She wrapped her hands around the canteen and took a long pull, like an alcoholic getting his drink on. She passed it to Lane, who did the same. They drank a quarter of the canteen, leaving the rest for the journey.

Together, they set off down the trail they'd crawled up the night before, traversing the overgrowth cautiously, and eyeing the welcoming pavement down below.

"I hope you're being careful, Alayna," Lane continued the game. "Otherwise this big, strong man will have to carry you down the mountain. And I don't think you want that. Do you?"

"Oh, he can take me in his arms whenever he pleases," Alayna said.

Clay knew this was truthful, yet it was edged with sarcasm. He rolled his eyes, trying to come up with his own jokes.

"You girls better watch it. You don't want to be on the wrong side of history."

"Ha. We already are," Alayna said.

Clay swallowed, realizing his joke rang true. "Fair point."

"What do you think will happen with all the

crazed when we destroy them with the device?" Alayna asked Lane, stepping over a bush. A few twigs peppered the ground.

"I'm really not sure," Lane said. "I imagine them falling all over each other, all at once. Making little hills of humanity's mistake."

"I hate that they were all once people. Like us. We've done our best to show mercy to the people who were going to transition, the ones that we knew," Alayna said. "But everyone else. I mean, imagine. Some of our neighbors. Some of our friends."

"We don't know who's crazed and who isn't, yet," Clay said, his voice stern.

He hated that he showed his irritation, his fear, so readily. Thoughts of Maia and Valerie once again floated to the surface. Silence hung between them as they trotted onto the road, all three minds hunting for a different topic. The truth was, the apocalypse was never far from their minds.

"Damn, Clay. I think you have even more muscles than you did last night," Lane commented.

Clay had already pulled ahead of them, hardly able to slow his feet. Taking a deep breath, he pulled up.

"These nanites. Wish I had them when I was training for that sprint marathon last year."

"You didn't even train!" Alayna said, laughing.

"I ran five miles. Once," Clay admitted.

"And then you ate like three donuts that morning."

"So did you," Clay said, giving her a pointed look.

"We didn't have a whole lot to care about back then, besides pastries. We were like the cops from the Simpsons. All we ever did was put people in jail for unnecessary kissing. How foolish does that sound now?"

They continued down the road, chatting amicably, the girls trying to keep their minds away from hunger. Clay hadn't felt a single pang, although he did have a persistent daydream about eating a hamburger with extra cheese. He imagined the juices dripping down his face, then Maia laughing at him, at his commitment to gobbling the patty in just a few bites. He envisioned Valerie telling Maia she would never get away with eating like such a slob.

"I would destroy one of those burritos from the midtown diner," Alayna said, clearly having her own food thoughts. "They weren't authentic Mexican, no. But they could slather cheese on a tortilla over there, and that's all I really want right now. Megan wouldn't let me eat them very often. Said they would make me fat. I wouldn't mind being fat right now," she chortled.

"Ha. I think I'd eat onion rings, if I could," Lane said. "Deep-fried, with dipping sauce. Oh, god. Just thinking about it is making my mouth water."

"Of course, Clay doesn't need food," Alayna said. "Not with the nanites in his blood."

"He's so lucky. I feel like I might die in five minutes."

"Yeah, well. I may very well die in just a few days from these parasites," Clay said, shuddering. He halted, turning toward the girls, his eyes panicked. "We'll get you your food. Your water. It's going to be all right for you. But it won't necessarily be all right for me. Do you get that?"

The women glanced at one another, seemingly speaking a language they'd cultivated together in the mere minutes Clay had left them alone that morning. Alayna shrugged slightly, as if to say, "There's no good way to handle this."

"I think we should take a break," Lane said, breaking the tension. "All this talk about burritos is making me crazy. Plus, we've been walking for . . . what? Three hours? That's more than my normal workouts before the apocalypse."

"Isn't it funny that we ever tried to keep those gym memberships?" Alayna asked, laughing and sinking to her knees on the pavement. "I mean, of all the things you could do in your life, why would you spend so many hours at the gym? It seems pathetic, now. If only someone had told me."

"It's okay, Alayna. I don't think you spent too much time there." Clay humored them. "I seem to remember quite a few nights where you and I snuck out for a beer or three before heading home. You didn't head to the gym. You lived."

"Or at least, I tried to," Alayna said.

"That's all we can really ask for," Lane agreed.

After a short break, during which they gulped as much water down as they could, they started again, guided by the confident movements of Clay—their leader, whether they liked it or not. And perhaps, since the morning's conversation—and since Clay had rebuffed Alayna again sexually—they were leaning toward the "not." Especially Alayna.

Clay could sense it. Alayna's resentment was nearly palpable, alongside the hunger and the fatigue. He was growing stronger than ever, leaving them further and further behind—sometimes literally. Once, infuriated, Alayna threw a stone at him. It bounced, stinging his skin. He turned around, his eyes violent and bright, making him appear almost machine-like.

"What the hell?" he asked, his voice low. "What

was that for?"

"You're like twenty feet in front of us," Alayna said, her eyes narrowed. "I don't know what kind of fucking leader you think you are. But this isn't what it means in my book."

Clay waited for them. The girls caught up, then pushed ahead of him, stride by stride. Clay followed, not wanting to make any more waves. He wanted to say something tart to Alayna, but held his tongue.

There was too much at stake. The world was spinning far too quickly. "Feelings" were irrelevant. And that's what he should have told Alayna the night before, when she'd pressed herself so insistently against him and asked him to be with her.

30.

After more breaks and countless rounds of half-bickering later, the three survivors crested a hill and viewed something miraculous, something that now seemed outside of time. It was Dearing, the first signs of it anyway: scraggly houses on the outskirts, water tower, and its grid lines of the inner city—probably named for all the trees in the forest, much as it was in the towns they had grown up in, in the towns they were from.

"God, it looks dead," Alayna gasped, scrutinizing the town below. It was as if they were on the deck of a ship, looking out over the water. But no fish skimmed the surface; nothing made a dramatic leap.

"I'm terrified," Lane said, looking at the road sign identifying the town and its population. "I never thought I'd be so scared of a silly little town. But look at me now. My fingers are trembling."

They were. When Lane extended them, her entire hand shook, like a drunk's. Her eyes were laced with tears, showing her fear, like a child. As her lip quivered, Clay seemed to grow taller, more confident, almost oblivious to their fear. He gazed down at them from his ivory tower of strength, certain they could feel it pumping within him.

"It's all going to be fine," Clay stated. "We have to

think positive."

"Yeah. You've got those nanites cranking away," Alayna said sarcastically. "Just try to imagine how we feel, won't you? For once?"

Clay raised his hands, feeling like the villain. "All I know is, we spent the better part of today walking all this way. Do you want to just turn back now?"

Lane reached for the canteen. She began to gulp at the water, as if she thought it might be the last she'd ever get. Her hands still shook. Alayna accepted the canteen next, drinking with similar zeal.

"Listen, if we don't go down there, then we'll never know. We'll never figure out what happened to our friends and family. We'll always wonder. Alayna—what about Megan?"

Alayna didn't stop drinking.

"And if we don't go on, then we may never find food. I could go on without it. I don't need it. I don't even want it," Clay lied, even as memory of that burger—a symbol for real life—hounded him. "But this is literally our only plan. Our only choice. And we've come all this way."

Lane and Alayna turned angry eyes on him. The canteen hung at Alayna's side, empty. Nobody spoke for several seconds, as they came to the realization that Dearing was in fact their only hope.

"We should have the neutralizer out at all times," Alayna said. "Like you said. If there are crazed in there, I don't want them to hear our gunfire."

"Agreed," Lane said. "But which one of us should . . ."

"She should take it," Alayna said, tipping her head toward Lane. "We'll have our guns drawn, just in case the first line of defense fails us."

Lane asked, "So, what's the general plan after

that, then?"

"We look for signs of life," Clay said firmly. "This can't be rocket science anymore, Lane. It can't be exact."

Lane's face was angry, but she remained silent.

Clay turned toward the city, unperturbed. He couldn't worry whether they were irritated with him, now. Not any longer.

"Shall we?" he asked. He sounded like he had after Maia had had temper tantrums as a child. He'd be taller, firmer, stoic. Showing her that no matter how loud she screamed, how hard she kicked, he still had the upper hand.

"Fine," Alayna said, taking a first step forward. With a fluid motion, she drew her gun, pointing it in front of her, making her look demonic, strong. "Those fuckers better stay away from me. I'm too irritated not to blow each and every one of their heads off."

31.

As they strode into Dearing, Clay knew it was going to be just as abandoned as Helen and Carterville before that. His heart sank further when against the wall of a small gas station, he saw a line of graffiti, "FML."

Clay remembered when he'd had to chase off graffiti artists back in Carterville. They'd just been kids who'd brought spray paint to the high school and put their distorted opinions over the whitewash. At the time, he barely made an effort to track them down—it would have been pointless and the paperwork was a hassle.

And, now, Clay felt it was fair to assume that whoever had written "FUCK MY LIFE" on that gas station wall was dead. No longer dissatisfied with their existence. He or she was completely absent. They had nothing.

"Any idea where anything is around here?" Alayna asked in a small voice.

"No clue," Clay said. "In all our years in Carterville, Val and I rarely stepped foot out of town. Let alone traveled this far south."

"Shit," Lane grumbled from the other side. "Do you want to check in the gas station for food?"

"I don't want to waste any more time," Clay

replied, still tracing the vacant city streets ahead.

But the girls were already advancing toward it and away from Clay, their weapons still drawn. The shadows were long on the buildings, turning them a ghoulish shade of blue. Lane barged into the half-destroyed convenience store, using her shoulder to push the door free of the debris blocking it. The place was lined with rubble from a raid, but the far back wall still had a few bags of snacks and some stale crackers. Alayna tore open a bag of almonds and shoved a large handful into her mouth. She chewed loudly, looking like an animal. Clay guarded the girls' plundering from near the front door and his heart twinged at Alayna's desperation—the way she ripped into the food, dropping crumbs on her shirt. She was no longer just a woman. She was a monster.

And so was he.

Lane took a bag of peanuts and chewed hungrily before shoving two little packs into her pocket. They drank two bottles of water each, tossing one to Clay and telling him to drink up.

"I'm good for now," Clay said, tossing the bottle back to the girls. "You two need this more than I do."

"The nanites won't make up for everything, Clay," Lane said flatly. "You still have to take care of your human needs."

Begrudgingly, Clay ate a pack of animal crackers and sipped the water, hating that they were losing time. Checking his watch, he realized they'd only been at the station for five minutes—maybe less than that. Time was moving strangely, with minutes like hours and days like years. It was like being a kid again.

After Alayna and Lane had had their fill, they turned to Clay, knowing it was time to move on.

Energized, at least briefly, they backtracked onto the road, flanking Clay down the middle of the street.

The town revealed its personality gradually, with fast food joints becoming sit-down diners—chain clothing stores turning into boutiques. The sun dropped closer to the horizon, increasing the town's eerie appearance. The businesses were completely deserted; the restaurants seemed to have been abandoned midway through a meal. Pressing their faces against the windows, they saw molding plates scattered across the tables.

"To have your life ruined during breakfast!" Lane said, trying to make a joke. "What kind of cruel world is this?"

"A world where scientists tried to play God," Clay said sarcastically. Lane didn't offer a reply.

Occasionally, one of them would dart toward the door of a random business or office building, hoping to find someone, anyone, hiding out inside. Someone unwilling to abandon their family-owned business, and decided to stay behind, hidden. Maybe someone had been spared while the rest of the city was ravaged.

"Looks like we might be too late," Alayna said, her voice distant.

"We can't give up," Clay replied.

"But if we could just rest for the night, we could get up tomorrow, maybe go back to the gas station for more supplies—"

"Wait," Clay interrupted her.

"I just don't think you're seeing reason. Maybe it's the nanites. Maybe it's your wife, your daughter—"

"Wait, I said," Clay growled. His eyes were on something in the distance. Blood pounded against his eardrums, nearly drowning out Alayna's protests. He saw a flash, some movement—it almost felt like he was staring into a concentration of ants, all of them moving in a strange, organic way, as they tried clamber in.

"Shit. It's them," he said.

He ducked behind a building, holding his rifle high. "It's the crazed."

"Where?" Lane whispered, peering off into the distance. "I can't see anything."

"By that hotel. About ten blocks up."

"How can you see that far?" Alayna was incredulous.

"Nanites, of course," Lane answered. "What else?"

They waited for several moments, hearing only their labored breathing. Clay peeked around the corner at the modest hotel, with its four or five stories and large windows, each of which had been covered with curtains. Squinting, he saw that the crazed were trying to get into the hotel, meaning that . . .

"There must be people inside," he said. "Survivors like us."

"How many of them are there?" Lane asked.

"Several dozen, at least," Clay said.

"Shit. We haven't had that many since just after we left Carterville," Alayna said. "And back then, we were more than just three people."

"Back then, we didn't have the neutralizer," he corrected. "And I don't think we really have a choice." He leaned close to Alayna, looking almost menacing himself—like one of the crazed had taken over his body for a split second—and he whispered harshly, "My daughter might be in there. Let's not forget why we're out here."

Alayna nodded, her movements almost imperceptible, and then took a dramatic step back, her skin almost green.

Time was running out.

32.

As they approached the hotel, Alayna and Lane were quiet, seeing what Clay had described to them in full detail now: the crazed, clambering over one another, tearing at the door.

"You think there're people inside?" Alayna asked. "The ones they shipped down from Helen? It's certainly big enough. It must have been used for—I mean. It would have been logical to house them up here."

"Keep them all in one place. For safety," Clay agreed. "We would have done the same, if we'd kept them all in Carterville."

"How the hell are we going to get in?" Alayna asked, ducking behind a corner, and peering toward the horde. "They haven't noticed us yet, which I guess is good. But it's only a matter of time."

Lane looked stunned. She hadn't faced the crazed like this . . . ever. Adjusting the neutralizer, her eyes darted from Clay to Alayna, clearly showing what little confidence she had in herself.

"With the neutralizer, we won't need to fight them the way we did before," Clay said, taking it from Lane's quivering hands.

Lane nodded, pressing her lips together and swiping her hair behind her ears. It was greasy, a shiny black in the growing darkness. "Shit. Okay. So, you're going to just go up to them and . . . obliterate the fuckers?"

"I suppose so." Clay turned his eyes to the hotel. He no longer knew what fear felt like. "Wait here."

He stepped out of their shadowy hiding spot and charged ahead, pointing the neutralizer at the crazed, squeezing the trigger rapidly. As he got closer, he began to swing it from side to side, as if fanning the invisible death rays across the swarm. Then, one by one, the crazed began to fall. First, dropping to their knees, then face planting on the pavement. They died without gunfire or blood spatter. In a way, he felt he was honoring the memory of their previous existence—ensuring they didn't end as gore plastered across the hotel windows.

But after a dozen or so shots, a red light started blinking. As he was nearly upon the diminishing mob, he looked down at the device, confused, his mouth agape.

"The fuck?" he wailed, shaking the neutralizer. He continued to squeeze the trigger—again and again—still knocking the crazed down, but at a much slower rate.

"Hey! Clay!" Lane cried, using her hands as a megaphone.

Clay whipped around. Why on Earth was she calling him now? Was she oblivious to the racket she was making?

"You need to let it recharge longer between each use!" she yelled.

Clay was filled with sudden anxiety. Why the fuck hadn't she told him that to begin with? Jesus. He'd wanted to give her more credit, but it was becoming more difficult with each passing moment.

Frustration brimming, Clay began to mash the trigger more ferociously, not caring what Lane said. He watched as the crazed continued to fall, a heap of the dead near the steps of the hotel. Some of the crazed had become aware of his presence and had turned their growling heads toward him, their eyes flashing with hunger.

"Hey," they seemed to say to one another, almost gossiping. "Let's just eat him, instead!"

It was as if they'd just decided on a different restaurant and given up on their current reservation. The pack began to advance toward Clay, making his stomach clench. The device worked exactly three more times, destroying two men in matching blue sweaters and an older, haggard-looking woman, with straggly blonde hair.

And then, the neutralizer stopped. No lights, no hum. Just a useless piece of technological junk in his hand.

"FUCK!" he yelled, whipping it across his shoulders and reaching for his gun. He began to fire at their heads, but he couldn't shoot fast enough. Dozens of them were still scrambling toward him; having completely abandoned their attack on the hotel. Clay could almost feel their gnawing, browning teeth on his arms, could almost sense what it would be like to transition, fully, into a monster.

He was almost there, anyway.

Suddenly, he heard the roar of gunfire echoing in from behind him. He saw Alayna's slim silhouette approaching, her gun drawn. She charged at the swarm, blasting away, disembodying the crazed nearly as fast as her running legs could stretch. She looked athletic, like a tiger barreling toward her prey.

Clay continued to shoot as well, causing various

shades of blood to paint the side of the hotel. Lane huddled somewhere behind them, unarmed and out of sight.

After a small eternity, Clay and Alayna came together near the center of their handiwork, dead crazed at their feet. They still clung to their guns, hands numb from firing. Neither spoke for several moments. Men and women were stretched over one another, becoming human again in death.

"Son of a bitch. I don't know how much more of this I can take," Alayna gasped, slinging her gun over her shoulder.

"I thought the neutralizer would make this easier," Clay said.

"That recharging bullshit?" Alayna said, chortling slightly. "Yeah. I didn't expect that."

"Can't blame her, I guess. She didn't know how rough it would be out here."

Alayna didn't reply. They heard Lane trotting up behind them, panting, clearly appalled at the blood and murder before her.

"Jesus," she gasped raggedly. "This is a nightmare."

The words were so understated that Clay had to force himself not to laugh. But death had become almost comical, now that he'd grown so accustomed to it. He supposed you could get used to anything. Even the apocalypse.

33.

Alayna stepped forward with a burst of renewed energy, planting a boot squarely mid-pane of the entry door panel. Clay whistled, impressed, as the glass shattered, revealing the maroon-colored carpet of the hotel lobby and a winding staircase beyond. It was a once-gorgeous place—a destination for those coming to Dearing, and had probably been built over a hundred years before.

"Let's go inside, shall we?" Alayna said, walking away from the pile of corpses. "I don't want to stick around for one of them to wake up again. Or for the smell to attract their friends." She stepped through the now ventilated entrance.

As Clay reached the door, he found Alayna standing frozen just inside the lobby. He slipped his rifle from his shoulder. He held it at the ready as stepped across the threshold. Once inside, he scanned the immediate area, taking in the surroundings.

"The survivors were here, all right," Alayna said, her voice a stark contrast to the solitude of the abandoned hotel. "But I don't think they're here anymore."

At the far side of the lobby was an auditorium and what appeared to be the dining room. Each was filled with countless mattresses and cots, with single sheets and sad-looking, lumpy pillows. Food waste, in the form of wrappers and old chip bags, littered the interior. Holding his breath, Clay tried to listen into the depths of the hotel—hoping to get a sense of whether there were people upstairs. But he heard nothing.

Alayna and Lane joined him, leaning heavily against the staircase rail. Blood was beginning to trail down Alayna's left cheek, a departing gift from the crazed.

"So they were here?" she asked hoarsely. "Do you think they left in a hurry?"

"It would seem so. Everything seems to be in a rush these days." He entered the auditorium, walking between the rows of cots. Would he recognize Maia's bunk if he saw it? Would she leave anything behind—anything he would know?

It had been so long since he'd seen her, since he'd held her. A depressing thought suddenly overwhelmed him: would he even know her face if he saw it?

"We should search the entire property. Don't you think?" Alayna said from the doorway. "I don't think we should assume anything from this one empty room. They certainly could have used the rest of the hotel."

"Sure," Clay said, nodding slowly. "But I think we should stick together. For all we know, one of the crazed might have gotten in. They could be hiding anywhere." His glanced at Lane, as an image—perhaps a premonition—appeared in his mind. Popping into a room, unaccustomed to the fighting and blood of this post-apocalyptic world, she'd find a crazed latched on her neck in no time. She'd fall to her knees immediately, her crimson blood becoming a horrific accent on the white walls.

Jesus. No. After all they'd been through, he couldn't allow it to happen. Not like that. He had to protect them.

"Up the stairs, then?" Alayna asked, pulling him from his reverie. She gripped the staircase railing and bounded up the steps. "This place gives me the creeps. The sooner we know what happened here, the sooner we can move on."

Clay and Lane joined her on the second floor landing, looking up and down the hallway. The carpet was old-fashioned, patterned, as if it had been styled for the turn of the 19th century. Clay imagined that Maia would have been fascinated with it, probably even thinking that when all this was over, she'd want her bedroom changed. She'd always liked odd, old-fashioned things, things that reeked of a time past, a time she hadn't known. She'd poured through old movies as a younger girl, things like Casablanca and An American in Paris.

Clay had teased her at the time, for not liking "normal things." But he'd actually loved this about her, telling Alayna often that his daughter was "going somewhere, someday." That she would find more out of life than he had, as a simple man with a basic job in a quiet town.

He wanted more for her.

Alayna opened the first room. "Nothing in here. Although it does appear that they were sleeping up here, too. Looks lived-in. More food wrappers left behind."

"Anything to eat?" Lane asked.

"Just packaging, mostly."

Clay peeked in. The blankets were stripped to the

base of the bed, showing that whomever had slept there hadn't liked to tidy up. Or maybe they'd left in a hurry.

"It must have been horrible, to come all the way here and think you were safe," Lane said.

Clay frowned, moving on and checking other rooms on the floor. Each was similar, with sheets stripped to the ground, as if they'd left in a hurry—flinging themselves from bed.

"Third floor, then," Alayna sounded less and less hopeful. "We aren't going to give up till the whole place is checked." She put a hand on Clay's back, showing a bit of compassion—despite feeling so disgruntled toward him earlier. "We have to keep fighting for this. And we will, Clay. For your daughter. And for Megan."

Lane nodded behind her, her jaw clenched tight. "No giving up."

"Worst case, we found shelter for the night," Clay said, taking to the steps. "A silver lining, if nothing else."

But his heart was growing heavy. His fists clenched, nails digging deeper into his skin, nearly drawing blood, vengeance in his eyes.

34.

The third floor offered nothing. Just more empty rooms, more comforters tossed back, with trash in the wastebaskets and empty water bottles tossed into corners. For a time, the people who'd stayed there, the people who had found safety there, had at least had food, water, and shelter.

"Why on Earth did they leave such a good situation?" Alayna asked. "And it's pretty clear that the crazed didn't get in. I mean. There'd be evidence of that. We'd see the blood. Possibly body parts riddled with bullet holes."

Clay nodded his head in agreement. They hadn't found a single sign of struggle, nothing to indicate that people had died in the hotel.

"It's confusing," Clay said. "Maybe they were taken up to Earlton after all, or maybe someplace else?"

"So, just another dead end," Lane whispered.

"For every dead end we find, we'll always find another trail," Alayna said, her eyes hopeful as she looked up at Clay. "We have one more floor to check, and then we can rest. Regroup. Okay?"

"Agreed," Clay said as he began to climb to the fourth floor.

The top floor was more of the same, until they

reached the end of the hallway furthest from the staircase. There, the door was covered over with dark paneling and screwed to the wall, almost hiding the fact that there was a door there at all.

Clay ran his hand across the wood, feeling the rough edges against his skin. "What the hell are they hiding behind here?" he asked.

"I don't know if we should go in," Lane said. "I mean, if everyone bugged out because of whatever's behind that door . . . I just don't think it's a good idea."

But Clay had already begun to rip the paneling from the wall with his now superhuman strength. With three quick jerks, the panel broke free and clattered to the floor. He shoved it aside with his foot before gripping the now exposed doorknob. Exhaling sharply, he twisted the handle and flung the door open.

His jaw dropped.

The room was laid out much like the others: with a four-poster bed, a large wardrobe, and piles of debris and other foodstuff along the walls. But lying on the filthy mattress, was a teenage boy—around fifteen or sixteen—tied to the bedposts. He was dressed in a pair of jeans and a black t-shirt. He was extremely thin, bones poking from his t-shirt, his arms stretched above his head. A putrid, urine scent met Clay's nose—the boy had soiled himself. Darkness stained his crotch area and the sheets, which had also been sweated through.

"Jesus Christ," Alayna whispered. She brought her hand to her mouth, almost unable to proceed.

Clay stepped in, concern on his face. Snot and mucus ran in thick trails from his nose to his mouth, and his eyes were closed. He was either sleeping, unconscious, or dead. Dark circles shadowed his eyes, nearly to his nostrils.

In that moment, Clay understood: this boy was a monster, a crazed. He'd been locked away because of his altered state. Perhaps he'd been someone's beloved son. Maybe he'd been a good brother, a kind friend. Clay swung his rifle around, pointing it at the boy's temple.

He needed to put him out of his misery. Now, and without prejudice. Standing there, as the seconds ticked away, he remembered all the people he'd seen go wild in the weeks since the outbreak. He should have shot them immediately as well, so as not to infect the others. He should have ended this the very day the outbreak had begun inside of his own jail cell. If only he'd listened to the colonel.

He could have saved the world with a single shot.

Aiming at the boy—the crazed monster—Clay took a deep breath, ready to fire.

"Wait!" Lane cried out, shoving past Alayna. Suddenly, she wasn't the meek woman she'd been downstairs. She put herself between the barrel of the gun and the rail-thin boy. "Wait. I think we should check and make sure he's actually infected."

"Can't you see it?" Clay asked, reacquiring his target. He didn't realize he was panicking. His eyes were manic, wild. "I need to put it down, now. It needs to leave this world."

"No," Lane insisted. "Not. Until. We. Check. Him."

Suddenly, the boy's eyes flickered open. Clay raised his rifle. The boy blinked once, then twice, revealing bloodshot, human, eyes.

"Help," the boy rasped through cracked lips. "Please. Help me."

Clay's heart nearly skipped a beat, and he lowered his rifle. He blinked, trying to make sense of what he was seeing. Was he imagining it?

Lane hurried to the boy. Clay slung his rifle over his shoulder and leaned heavily against the bedpost. The boy's panic was muted by his appalling condition, and his words were almost dreamy.

"What happened to you?" Alayna asked him, not daring to touch him. She stood a foot away, her eyes wide.

"I—I don't—" he stuttered. "I—I—can't—"

"He's delirious."

"But is he infected?" Clay asked. "It looks as if he's in the initial stages. Can you tell?"

"Hey, can you hear me? Have you been bitten?" Lane asked, gazing into his eyes with all the compassion of a mother. "Can you tell us what's going on? We can help."

What if they couldn't? Clay thought. He closed his eyes, waiting the final fall of the ax.

"I—I'm not—" the boy stuttered. "Please—Help me . . ."

Clay and Alayna shrugged at each other. Lane leaned closer, whispering, "What's your name, kid?" She reached forward, making her first physical contact, feeling his forehead.

"Alex," he breathed. "It's Alex."

35.

C lay leapt forward and began to untie the ropes. Alex. The kid's name was Alex.

He was coherent enough to remember who he was, that he had a past. He was a person, not at all one of the crazed. And someone had tied him to this bed. And left him to die.

The ropes were wrapped multiple times, with the strength of sailor knots. Alayna started at Alex's ankles. Lane continued to mop sweat from the boy's forehead, muttering to herself the whole time.

"We need to get him cleaned up. Now," she said, unaffected by the putrid smell.

That stench seemed to grow worse with each passing moment. Clay paused to swipe the back of his hand across his mouth, sensing he was on the verge of vomiting. Alayna was a pale shade of green. Their eyes met across the boy's rail-thin body, both holding the same truth.

"One second." Alayna headed for the doorway. She disappeared down the hallway, the sound of retching echoing back to them.

"You gonna do the same?" Lane asked Clay.

"No. No," Clay said, hoping it was true. He finished the last of the restraints, releasing Alex's ankle. His skin was livid underneath. The boy's eyes had closed again, but he continued to sweat, causing him to shiver.

"We need to get him out of these clothes. Immediately," Lane said.

Alayna appeared, carrying new sheets and pillows. She tossed them to the side of the bed then instinctively wiped her mouth, clearing the last of the vomit. "Sorry about that," she said, unable to look at either of them. "Just lost it for a minute."

Clay slipped his hand behind Alex's shoulders, helping him ease forward. Alex coughed, his chapped lips growing whiter with each heave. Clay eased his legs over the side of the bed.

"He won't be able to hold his own weight." He eyed Alayna. "Can one of you—"

Alayna stepped forward, taking Alex's other side and pulling him to his feet. He slumped over and leaned heavily against Clay's shoulder, his arms hanging like twigs. Clay remembered photographs of concentration camp survivors he'd seen in antiquated history books: carved out cheekbones, lost eyes. Alex resembled them perfectly.

As Alex clung to Clay, Lane busied herself undressing him, with the air of a hospital nurse. She tugged at his soiled pants and then folded them for later disposal. She pulled his shirt over his head, undoing one arm after the other, and then turned in a swift motion and yanked the sheets from the bed, revealing the piss-stained mattress beneath.

"All right then," she said, her voice bright and cheery. "Let's get these new sheets on. And get him cleaned up." She looked at Alayna.

"How?" Alayna asked. "There's no water in the hotel. I just tried down the hall."

"Check the toilets," Lane said firmly.

Clay picked him up, carrying him like a child. The hotel room had a bathroom behind a closed door. When they opened it, they revealed an antique, gold-edged mirror on the far wall, which reflected manic-eyed Clay, the anxious and still green-tinged Alayna, and Alex, in Clay's arms reeking of sickness and death.

Alayna grabbed a basin from the sink and then begin to scoop the water from the toilet into it, as Clay eased Alex onto the counter. A washcloth, still new, hung in the shower. She grabbed it, dipping it into the water, and then began to wash him with a tentative hand.

Clay watched as Alayna's washcloth moved from the boy's crotch to his feet, using the soap to make suds, eliminating the grime. Slowly, the stench was fading, allowing both Alayna and Clay to breathe through their noses again. Clay helped clean him then, taking a large towel and mopping at Alex's head. With each dab of the towel against his face, Clay was reminded of all the times Maia was ill, sweat on her forehead and her eyes searching her father's—begging for him to make her better.

Lane appeared in the doorway. "The sheets are back on. I tossed the dirty clothes and sheets into the corner. I didn't want to throw it out to attract the crazed. How's he doing?"

"Just about got him clean," Alayna said, focused on her work.

"I have about a million questions for him," Clay added.

The boy blinked up at him, almost on cue.

"I want to know whether or not he knew Maia." Clay stared directly into his half dead eyes.

"Clay," Lane said, hesitating. "I don't think you

should. I think it's too soon."

"He was coherent enough to tell us his name," Clay insisted. "He should be able to tell us something. Anything else. Hey. Alex. How did you come to be here? Who was here with you? Did they tell you where they were going?"

Alex's head lolled to the side, resting his cheek against the mirror. "Ummm . . ." he murmured, then began muttering to himself. "They were here. There they were. All . . . here."

"Who was all here?" Clay pressed. "Was someone named Maia?"

"Clay," Lane warned. "He's too sick for this."

"Dammit. We're all too sick for this," Clay retorted.

Alayna cleaned the last of the grime from Alex's face, tossing the dirtied washcloths and towels into the bathtub. Alex continued to shiver uncontrollably, looking moments from passing out again.

"Let's get him back to bed," Lane said, stepping back into the hotel room.

Clay scooped him up and carried him back to fresh, clean sheets and eased him onto the mattress. Lane tucked him in, then pulled the comforter up to his neck.

"That's okay, Alex," she soothed. "It's going to be all right. We'll get you better, won't we?"

His body continued to tremble for several moments. Alayna and Clay glanced at one another, with Clay's thoughts centered only on what information he could get out of the kid, knowledge that could possibly reunite him with his daughter. They had to keep him alive if only for that.

"Who were you with, kid?"

Lane gave Clay a dark look.

Alex's eyes popped open. His lips parted.

"Give him water," Clay said. "Now."

Alayna rushed back to the bathroom, filling an empty hotel cup with toilet water, and delivering it to Alex. They watched as the boy gulped the water greedily.

Licking his lips, Alex hunted for words. "Who the . . . who are you?" he asked, his voice raspy. He looked fearful, his eyes yellowed.

"We're here to help," Lane reassured him. "We cleaned you up. You're very sick. Try to stay calm."

"I don't know you." Alex's his eyes darted from face to face. "But I—I don't know anyone anymore."

"You were here with someone. They tied you up," Clay said, lifting Alex's head so he could drink more water. "We just need a bit more information from you. We need your help. Can you try and help us?"

Alex nodded, seemingly trying to focus his thoughts. "I was with a . . . some others," he whispered. "People. Survivors. That's what we call ourselves now, isn't it? We survived something. At least, we have so far."

"Why'd you stop here?" Alayna asked.

"Food. Shelter. The hotel had it," Alex continued. He dropped his head to the pillow. "But there were others here already."

Alex's eyes began to droop. Clay put his hand on the boy's shoulder, and started to shake him.

"Don't, Clay. He needs to rest," Lane said.

"We don't have time. We need to find out as much as we can."

"We can't get anything from him if he dies on us," Lane retorted.

But Clay continued to shake the boy, insisting he wake. "Hey. Kid. Alex. Who was in the hotel already? Other survivors? Do you remember any of their names?"

Alex's eyes popped open. "We—we weren't here very long," he murmured. "Not long. Before they came. The dead . . . monsters. They used to be people. They used to be just like us."

"And they escaped? They left you here to save themselves?" Clay demanded.

"The healthy. They got to leave. But me . . ." Alex started gasping for oxygen, before losing consciousness once more. His lips hung open, fish-like.

"Fuck," Clay yelled. He let go of Alex's shoulders and stormed to the far side of the room.

"Maybe he was left behind because he was too sick to travel," Lane suggested. "They must have thought he was going to turn. The symptoms are similar."

"This epidemic—that you all created—is a bit more common than the flu, these days," Clay interjected.

"Whatever," Lane snapped. "Regardless, he probably wasn't told much. Just tied up here to die. What kind of monster would do that?"

"One that was probably no better than those crazed wondering the streets," Alayna said, leaning against the bedpost.

"Alex. Hey," Clay said, shaking the boy's shoulders. "Alex. Wake up."

The boy blinked awake. He stared at them incredulously, as if searching his mind for recognition.

"Do you remember anyone else that was here? The other survivors? Can you remember their names?" Clay asked, his voice rising. "Anything.

Anything at all?"

"He doesn't remember, Clay. He's had the flu for who knows how long. You know what it's like to get the flu," Alayna said. "You're really out of it."

"Anyone's name, kid. Can you remember talking to anyone?"

"I—" Alex breathed. His eyes searched the ceiling, like a daydreamer. "Survivors? What a silly—" He pressed his lips together, licking what was left of the toilet water. "I—I miss her. She was—she was—" He paused. "M-Myy."

Clay jerked up, his heart thumping against his ribcage.

"What did you just say?" he demanded, wanting to know for sure.

"Mona—" Alex whispered, tailing off. "Mmaia."

His eyes closed. He took a long, gasping breath, and then fell into darkness—a deep sleep from which Clay couldn't awaken him. Not in that moment.

In the silence that followed, Clay's mind raced.

Maia. Jesus. Maia.

He'd heard only the name, and nothing more. Was she alive? Was she safe? Had she gone with the others, or had she—God forbid—been attacked?

His eyes swept the room, hunting for any clue of her. He wished he could smell her. Feel her presence. Know if she'd existed in that very room.

Alayna broke into his reverie. "We should let him rest for a little while, Clay."

"He knows her," Clay said. His head swung back and forth wildly, his fingers twitched. Could Alayna even understand how this made him feel? She wasn't a parent. She'd never even expressed any desire for children. She could never imagine the love for a child. This wasn't a game for him. This was his lifeblood.

This was his everything.

36.

L ane stepped in front of Clay.
        "No," she said, her voice low, like a growl.
"You're done here for now."

"You heard him," Clay exclaimed. "He said her name, Lane. Maia! Don't you understand what that means?"

"I understand that he's delirious," Lane said. "And it's quite incredible that he's even lived this long. You know, if we'd been just one day later, we would have found a dead body instead of a malnourished boy who was left for dead by people. People like us. We have to remember our humanity, Clay."

"Fuck humanity. He knows where she is," Clay snarled at Lane, jabbing her with his finger.

The motion was forceful, jarring Lane back slightly. Alayna gasped, and covered her mouth. A heavy silence followed.

Clearing her throat, Lane stood her ground. "I will not be bullied."

Clay felt a burning in his brain. He pulled his fingers through his hair, his shoulders shaking with anger. He realized he was out of line and knew he should apologize, but words would not form. He pointed at the dying boy.

"You have to save him, then," he said. "You have to make sure he lives. He knows Maia. He knows where they took her."

Alayna interrupted, "Clay! Just because he said her name doesn't mean he knows any of that."

Clay shook his head. "What do you mean?"

"She could just be the last person he remembers. Possibly not your Maia at all," Alayna said. "Just the last friend he had before they all packed up. And that doesn't mean he knows where they went. He might have been delirious when he was tied to the bed. It's actually a pretty sure bet. Right, Lane?"

Lane nodded, not looking at Clay. She placed a hand on Alex's forehead, checking his temperature. It seemed to radiate through the room, fueling all their nerves.

"If he knows anything about Maia, then that's all the more reason to save him." Clay folded his arms across his chest. He refused to believe that Alex knew nothing. They'd found him for a reason. Now, they'd save him. They were limping along from miracle to miracle. Weren't they?

"Well, I don't have the proper supplies," Lane said. "There's not a lot I can do for him here. I can keep him warm. Administer fluids. I don't have a great deal of hope, to be honest."

But Clay refused to believe it. He turned to the door, his mind already rolling. "Then we need to get to a hospital. Even though they're most likely abandoned, they must still have plenty of supplies. We could even stock up for the future."

"Well, of course," Lane said. "But Alex is in no condition to be moved. We could hardly handle moving him to the bathroom, let alone across town. And if we come across the crazed—"

"He would hold us back. Put us in jeopardy," Alayna said. "I agree with Lane. He needs to stay put."

"Then, you both stay here. Watch him," Clay grunted. "I'll head to the hospital. I think I saw it on the other side of the railroad tracks as we came into town. Shouldn't be more than a thirty minute walk."

"No. You're not going out there by yourself," Alayna protested. "I'll go with you. Lane can stay here. Watch over Alex. She's safe here. But out there—there's just no way we can know how many are out there, waiting for you. I don't want you to be surrounded."

Clay felt his heartbeat ramp up. He nodded slowly, knowing Alayna was right.

"We're losing time," Lane said, and began to describe the supplies she needed, scribbling them down on a piece of paper from her back pocket. She passed it to Clay, sounding breathless. "But shit, I almost forgot. The neutralizer. It needs a new battery."

Clay flipped his thumb toward the door, shrugging. "I'll just stop by the store on the way back. What size does it take?"

"You don't understand," Lane said. "It's a special kind of battery. Long life, high output. That sort of thing."

"You're saying we can't get it at the local supermarket, then?" Clay asked, incredulous. "Because that doesn't seem practical in this end of world scenario. I'm no rocket scientist here, but wouldn't it have made better sense to design the device to utilize a standard battery? I mean, assuming there are enough batteries in the world to power it up."

"It wasn't developed for this kind of emergency. It was designed for the military. They would have always had supplies . . ." she trailed off. The silence stretched between them, heavy with recriminations.

"As far as I know, there's no military base around here," Clay said, bringing his fist against his thigh. He immediately felt a bruise begin to form. He didn't know his own strength.

"Mobile defibrillators. At the hospital." Lane's eyes were dancing through computations or algorithms that only she could see. "They use a similar power source, if you can believe it. If you find one at the hospital, grab it. If all goes well, I should be able to make it work."

"And if you can't?" Clay asked.

The silence that followed was deafening.

"Fuck it," Clay said and shrugged. "Let's get a move on."

He passed through the open door and into the hallway, which reeked of Alayna's vomit. He marched toward the staircase, Alayna behind him. As the minutes ticked by, he knew Alex's death was nearing.

And with his death, Clay was afraid he would lose Maia for good.

37.

C lay bolted down the staircase with Alayna following. He didn't dare look back; she would see that he was near sobbing. His eyes were tinged red with a mix of anger and sadness and fear, knowing that with each passing moment, his daughter was inching away from him.

At the hotel entrance, where they'd shattered the window, he crunched through the glass. Alayna's voice calling out his name hardly registered.

"Clay! Hey! Clay," she cried. "Listen to me."

Clay paused at the doorway. "We don't have time to talk."

"But we don't have what we need to just leave like this," Alayna said, resting her hand on his shoulder in an attempt to ground him. His body twitched at her touch. "We need to look for weapons, ammunition, anything they could have left behind. If they were in such a hurry to leave, they might have left supplies, things we could use out there. Let's not go out there half-cocked, is all I'm saying."

Clay knew she was speaking reasonably. He sighed, and turned back toward the foyer. She eyed him fearfully.

"Let's split up, then," Clay said. "You take the upper floors, and I'll look down here. The kitchen.

The supply closets. Maybe there's a basement we missed. The hospital I saw was across town, but maybe there's a closer one. Find a phone book."

They separated, Alayna darting back up the stairs and Clay turning toward the wide swinging doors, which led him into the hotel kitchen with its bright countertops, scattered with food packaging. A large slab of meat rotted on the counter. The smell made Clay's stomach turn. Bolting through the room, he found a supply closet near the pantry. Inside, a dozen automatic weapons were positioned, lined up like library books. There were three flashlights and several boxes of ammunition on the shelf above.

"Fuck yeah." Clay reached for a gun and found the right ammo. He loaded—his movements deft and precise—as if he'd been at war his entire life.

Not like before, when he'd been a slightly overweight sheriff, just waiting to go home for the day. That Clay didn't seem to exist anymore.

He slipped two flashlights into front pockets then took another gun for Alayna before heading back to the foyer. As he looked down the countertop, past the slab of meat, he saw a few packages of granola bars in the corner. Grabbing them, he ripped his teeth into one of the packages, pulling out the snack, sugar tingling on his tongue.

In the foyer, Alayna was waiting for him, emptyhanded.

Clay tossed a pistol across the room. She caught it deftly, surprise on her face. "Is this loaded?" she asked. "It could've gone off."

"It didn't," Clay said. "You find a phone book?"

"Just the one hospital is listed. The one we saw coming in. I think that's our best bet. Where'd you get the firepower?" she asked, spying Clay's newly adorned holster.

"Supply closet through the kitchen." Clay thumbed over his shoulder.

"Anything else back there?"

"At least ten more. It's strange they left so much here. Oh. And I found these." He tossed a pack of granola bars toward her. She nabbed them from the air and ate them quickly, her jaw grinding like a wild animal. Clay looked away, he didn't like to see her like that.

The ingrained behavior of civilized society was dropping away from them. They were blood and guts and wants and needs. For all intents and purposes, they were animals with guns, on the loose in a jungle.

"You get enough?" Clay asked.

"It'll never be enough. Can't you see how much weight I've lost?" she asked, bits of granola falling from her lips. "I'll be skin and bones before the end of the week. We should get some up to Lane and the kid. He'll be needing fuel soon."

"Hurry," Clay snapped, pointing toward the staircase. "We leave in five."

Watching her scamper up the steps, he felt high, dominant, resilient. When Alayna reached the foyer once more, the food delivered, she was huffing, out of breath.

38.

The streets of Dearing were eerie, abandoned of anyone living or dead. It was long after sundown, and the few street lamps that still worked flickered like a cartoon haunted house, casting strange shadows. Clay and Alayna held their guns forward, scanning left and right. For a long time, as they crept through the town, they found no reason to speak.

Their path was crowded with abandoned cars, most of them stalled haphazardly, with several rammed into the backs of others—as if some kind of real-life bumper car ride had opened up to the general public. Clay and Alayna had to bob and -weave through the streets, darting between the wreckage, crunching over broken glass on the pavement.

As they moved, Clay peered into the abandoned cars, trying to make sense of the lives that were left behind. The effect was humbling. Car seats, empty—probably still sticky from bottles of formula or milk. Toys scattered throughout. Several of them resembled the little red sedan Valerie had driven when they'd first met as teenagers, all those years before. They'd made out in the back, finding all the uniquely wonderful ways they could make each other's bodies feel—unaware they were just animals, chasing hormones like dogs chase balls.

"It's weird not to see anyone in an entire town like this," Alayna said. "I don't think I'll ever get used to it."

"There's a lot we won't get used to," Clay said.

After nearly forty minutes, they reached the hospital, a two-level building made of concrete and steel. They approached the emergency room entrance first, peering into the long, whitewashed hallways. The automatic doors didn't open—no power. Alayna reached for a decorative rock near an overgrown bush. She prepared to hurl it through the glass.

"Don't!" Clay held his hands up. "That could attract them. We've been lucky so far, but who knows how long that'll last?"

Alayna nodded and dropped it to the cement walk with a dull crack. "Let's circle the building then. I'm sure there's another entrance."

"Agreed," Clay said.

They crept around the building, eyeing the dark, shadowed windows.

Alayna stopped short.

"What's the matter?" Clay asked, turning toward his one-time deputy.

"How are we going to see a thing in there? The power—"

Clay slipped the two flashlights from his pockets like a magician. "Voila!" he said, handing one to Alayna.

"Aren't you full of surprises." She clicked the power button on and off several times.

"I found them in the same storage closet where they stashed the guns and ammo. I figured it might get a little dark in there. It'd be tough to see things without them."

"Great thinking," Alayna said. "You don't think anyone's hiding out in there, do you? Waiting for fools like us to stumble in?"

"People could have used this as a shelter, sure. We just have to have our wits about us," Clay said. "They could try to shake us down, or worse, try to kill us. Desperate times. You can't say what anyone will do."

"Right."

They rounded another corner and found an auxiliary entrance, where a dark, narrow corridor led into the depths of the hospital. Alayna stayed behind Clay, her breath coming in ragged bursts, showing her fear. He clicked on his flashlight. It blinded them for a moment before their eyes adjusted.

"We'll need to find batteries for these at some point," Clay whispered. "I didn't see any back at the hotel."

"Let's head toward the front of the building," Alayna murmured, her voice quivering. "I think I saw a directory through the glass doors. It should show us where the pharmacy is. I don't want to waste time wandering around too much. This place gives me the major creeps. And that smell!"

The odor was a foul mix of unwashed bedpans and decomposition. Having come directly from Alex's room to this, it was easy to link horrible smells with fear. Even that first day in the jail cell, Clay had felt fear, had smelled the rank vomit and alcohol, and then had unknowingly contracted the infection.

This was an unclean world.

They made their way through the dark hallways, walking what seemed like miles, ending up in countless dead ends. They passed nurses' stations and dark, closed doors, until they finally found the facility's admissions center. The place looked orderly, with the clerk's chairs still facing their desks, almost as if everyone had just gone out to lunch and turned out the lights.

"There. The directory," Alayna said, pointing toward a large map of the premises. She traced her finger up and down, then across the floor plan, studying its layout before finally stabbing a finger on top of their destination. "Wing C. Didn't we pass a Wing C on the way here? About five minutes ago?"

"No," Clay said, eyeing the staircase. "Just A and B. I think you're looking at the second floor, there."

"Ah. Right," Alayna said, waving her flashlight over the map again. "It's directly above us."

Turning toward the staircase, they hurried up, a sudden bounce in Alayna's step—presumably from the much-needed fuel that the granola bars gave her. She surged past him, entering the darkness of the second-floor hallway first. Her confidence was stronger now than it had been less than an hour ago. Chances of finding any of the crazed seemed low.

Once in the pharmacy, however, their confidence bottomed out.

"Shit," Alayna said, kicking at an empty cardboard box and watching it bounce against the far wall.

The place had been cleared out. The shelves were bare, with boxes tossed to the floor. All the medication had been taken. The drawers in the pharmacists' desks had been yanked open, analyzed, sifted through.

"Think it was the people at the hotel?" Alayna asked.

"No way to know," Clay said. He raised his fist,

preparing to punch the nearest wall. Anger pulsed within him. "Come all this fucking way, and it's empty. And now the kid's going to die."

He allowed the silence settle around them. Alayna sighed. Her flashlight to dropped to her side, where it beamed a bright circle on the floor.

"But . . . these were only the meds that were being sold," she said, realizing.

"What do you mean?"

"The hospital must have NFR meds for their own internal use," Alayna said. "You know. Supplies they used to actually treat their patients. Everything that was in here was almost certainly for resale."

"Okay. Where would that be? I'm pretty sure it's not in the directory," Clay said.

"Near the emergency room for starters," Alayna replied. "Although it could also be near a nurses' station. I'm not sure . . ."

Clay turned back toward the staircase, and was back in the admissions center in minutes. The emergency room sign pointed down the hall. He moved quickly, heart pounding, his flashlight snaking across the floor ahead of him. The rank smell seemed to get worse as they approached the ward—perhaps indicating that the sick and injured had been left for dead when the crazed struck.

He didn't want to look into any of the rooms to check.

When they reached the emergency room nurses' station, they found it to be similarly ransacked. Boxes scattered on the floor. Cabinets completely cleared out. "Fuck," he yelled, his voice echoing.

"I don't really know . . . I mean, maybe we could check some of the pharmacies around town?"

They both knew the reality was that if the

hospital was ransacked, those places would be, as well.

Clay seethed with anger. He pushed ahead, opening as many of the doors as he could. They were all pilfered, with papers and empty boxes strewn around. It was almost artistic, the way every door led to more mess. It was a metaphor, perhaps, for this strange, new world. Every town they entered seemed to offer the same dreary, post-apocalyptic streets— the same crashed cars—the same familial memories. The same dead.

As he made his was down the hallway, he continued to open doors, feeling like a hunter. Alayna followed him, making skeptical noises.

"I just don't think we'll find anything, Clay. I don't want to waste our energy. Maybe we should just cut our losses? Head back to the hotel? Get an actual good night's sleep?"

"No. We can't have come all this way for no reason," Clay snapped. "We have to find something. Some kind of . . . anything." He tried another door, finding more of the same. He shivered, feeling the hopelessness descending like clouds.

"Fuck this," he said.

"Wait. Clay, look." Alayna pointed toward a dark, massive door at the far end of the hallway, broader than most of the others, with a small green badge near the handle. "It says—it says Internal Supplies."

Clay reached it in seconds, grabbing the knob and yanking it as hard as he could. But it didn't twist. The door didn't budge.

Clay gasped, pounding his fist against it. "Alayna, do you know what this means?" he asked. "It means we might have finally found some luck. If we can't get in there, neither could they. This—this could be our last hope."

Alayna put her hands on her hips, watching Clay as he considered the door. They shared a feeling of hopelessness. Their flashlights began to dim.

39.

C lay took several steps back and then lunged at the door, twisting his shoulder and slamming into it. The wood began to splinter, but it didn't give. Alayna was startled, dropping her flashlight to the ground. She was torn. Stare at Clay in disbelief or watch her flashlight roll off down the corridor.

"How'd you do that?" she asked.

Clay turned back, grinning broadly. "I think one more ought to do it, don't you?"

"The nanites," Alayna murmured. "Is that really what it is?"

"Who cares? It worked, didn't it?" He stepped back and then threw himself at the door again. It broke away, leaving the knob still locked in the jamb as it flew open. He shone his flashlight in, illuminating shelves of packaged medical supplies— two entire rooms of it, enough to stock the hospital for several weeks.

"It's all here, Alayna," he said. "All of it."

Alayna nabbed her flashlight and peeked in behind him, her eyes growing large. "Wow," she breathed, taking several steps in and beginning to read the labels. "This is all cancer medicine. Can you imagine having to deal with cancer at a time like this?"

For a moment, an image of a cancer-ridden crazed passed through Clay's mind: a large tumor growing from the monster's throat, his eyes secreting yellow puss. He shook the morbid thought away.

"Stock up on cold and flu medicine," he said. "And maybe some painkillers, just in case."

Alayna started reading labels and tossing things in her backpack. It filled quickly. After Clay offered her his bag, he meandered down the long aisles, looking for mobile defibrillators. His heart pounded, telling him they needed to hurry. They needed to get back to the kid. But without the defibrillators, their own survival was at stake.

Skirting around the far corner, he saw them. For a moment, he couldn't believe his luck. They'd wandered through the entire hospital, tearing open nearly every closet door, and here they were, all lined up in a row.

"Jackpot," he shouted, rubbing his palms together. He grabbed his second backpack and dropped in one of the four mobile defibrillators, then turned and found Alayna behind him, both her backpacks bulging with the meds.

"Only one?" she asked. "We'll need another for later. No clue how long they last. Why not grab them all?"

"They're actually quite heavy. I don't know if we can carry all of them along with the medical supplies," Clay said, his voice urgent. "Besides, if Lane can't get this to work, it'll all be for nothing. And if she does, we can come back for the rest of them."

Alayna nodded. "Fair point. But how about we take two just in case? I can handle these two backpacks, if you want to lug the two defibrillators."

"Sure," Clay said, yanking another unit from the

shelf. "Whatever you say, doc."

Alayna shook with sudden laughter, looking almost manic in the soft light of the flashlight. "I can't believe we found this stuff. We actually did what we set out to do. Do you remember the last time something worked out?"

Clay gazed at her fondly, if only for a moment. He began to reach forward, wanting to touch her shoulder—to tell her that things would get easier from here on out.

But before he touched her, they heard a howl in the distance. The blood drained from Alayna's face.

"What—what was that?" she stammered although they both knew exactly what it was.

"Great. We have company," Clay said grimly, pointing his flashlight back toward the hallway. "We better get out of here before we can't."

"And how do you think we'll manage that?" Alayna asked. "I hardly remember the way back to admissions."

"We'll manage, Alayna. We have to," he said.

They set off down the hallway, their weapons drawn and their ears sharp, watching for the crazed. They eased down the first hallway and then raced past the nurses' station, finding themselves deeper in the belly of the hospital.

"What time do you think it is?" Alayna asked, jogging alongside Clay.

"No idea," Clay said. "It was dusk when we arrived in Dearing. But that seems like a million years ago."

They continued down the hallway, getting increasingly lost. Clay led them down a series of turns, feeling certain that his path would take them toward the entrance. Instead he led them back to the same place—a sign that read, EAT HEARTY EAT HEALTHY, with a list of fruits and vegetables beneath.

"You'd better try," he said.

They heard another howl, much closer than they were comfortable with.

"I think I saw some light that way," Alayna whispered, pointing at the right fork of the maze. "Clay, I think it might be morning."

"Lead the way," he said.

They hurried toward the soft, grey light that seeped in through a distant window, which they reached after two more turns. The window cast long shadows on the hallway floor. Their eyes rose and waited to adjust to the change in brightness. They froze, filled with sudden panic. Clay's finger flicked against the trigger of his gun.

"There must be fifty of them," Alayna gasped.

In front of the doors, a horde of the crazed were plastered against the glass, pounding with bloodied fists. Their mouths were wide open, revealing toxic green gums, their eyes yellowed and puss-filled, and they were crying out some kind of animalistic chant. Clay tried not to look at their faces, knowing that in short order, they'd have to shoot them all in the head if they wanted to survive.

"We can't make it through that," Alayna said. "There's absolutely no way."

Both flashlights flickered out.

"Fuck," Clay snarled. "I guess we're really screwed now. We can't go back through the hospital without light, and we can't face that many of them head on."

The crazed growled, hammering their noses against the windowpanes until they bled.

"I think I'll take my chances in the dark," Alayna whispered.

"Maybe you're right."

They turned back toward the impenetrable darkness of the hospital, both grateful not to be staring death so squarely in the face. As they took their first steps into the corridors, the sound of rapid gunfire met their ears, growing louder.

"What the—" Clay turned around.

The bullets were coming from somewhere beyond the crazed—from someone crazy enough to take on a horde that large without batting an eye. One by one, the crazed convulsed before flailing to the ground in a miasma of blood and puss, their muscles twitching with their final throes. Realizing that the bullets were getting closer, Clay shoved Alayna to the ground and covered her with his body. The bullets began to impact the glass, shattering it into clouds of twinkling shards.

40.

"There. The reception desk. Get behind it," Clay said, pointing. He had no idea if the person shooting was their enemy. Not knowing if this world would be friendly to other survivors—he couldn't chance it knowing that someone had literally tied a teenage boy to a bed and left him to die.

That was the kind of world they were living in.

Alayna and Clay crawled toward the reception desk as the blasts grew louder, more insistent.

When they reached the safety of the desk, they hunkered down and waited as the barrage of gunfire continued. They didn't dare look out, for fear of being struck by a stray bullet themselves.

"What are we going to do when it's over?" Alayna whispered. Please, protect me, she seemed to ask. Save me.

The gunfire finally stopped. Clay peeked around the desk, blinking into the brightness of the new day. Several armed people were storming the steps of the hospital, their automatic weapons strapped across their chests and their motions sure. They looked like full-sized action figures from Clay's youth, ones he'd positioned on the windowsill and forced to tumble to the floor to their deaths.

The gunmen stepped over the threshold and into

the broken glass, their boots crunching. They didn't speak. Why weren't they talking? Clay's heartbeat ramped up, making them both shake. It was the adrenaline asking him, what are you going to do now?

He wasn't going to be a coward.

"Hey," he said, his voice booming. "Hey. Don't shoot. We're human back here."

He heard his voice bounce across the room. The gunmen cocked their weapons, clearly alert. The sounds of the clicking echoed in the stillness.

"I said don't shoot," he said again. "We're not the crazed. We're survivors." He waved the tips of his fingers over the counter, careful not to expose his face or head. "Please. Listen. We're human. We're from Carterville. We're just trying to stay alive."

The silence was heavy. Even with their own automatic weapons, they'd never be able to take all of them. They'd be blasted to the ground immediately, their bright red blood running across the linoleum. Their futures—finished.

Finally, the voice of a woman met his ears.

"Show yourselves," she demanded. "Immediately."

Clay grasped Alayna's upper arm, pulling her to her feet. They turned toward the voice. A woman and two men, all three holding automatic weapons. Pointed directly at Clay and Alayna.

"Don't shoot," Clay said, raising his hands high. Alayna followed suit. "We were just looking for medicine. A friend is sick. Real sick. He—he might not make it."

The woman jerked her head, sending one of her comrades to take their weapons. Clay watched helplessly.

"We really, really do need those to stay alive," Clay said. "How do you expect us to make it out there without guns?"

"And the backpacks," the woman said. "Take them, too."

The man relieved Clay and Alayna of their packs, including the one with the defibrillators, then walked back to the woman and the other armed man. Their eyes were blank.

"You don't understand," Clay tried.

"Thanks, but I think we need this more than you do." Her words were flippant. "I really, really do."

The men positioned themselves on either side of her, holding their weapons steady. The woman—tall, blonde, perhaps once beautiful, if that meant anything at all in this new, horrible reality, looked mere moments from laughter.

Clay and Alayna had become pawns, yet again. And it made Clay's blood boil.

41.

C lay's eyes narrowed, making him look capable of madness, of murder. He watched as the strange armed men took the supplies, the things that could have helped him to find his daughter again. His words were hoarse, illustrating his distress.

"You can't just take everything," he said. "I told you. We have to save our friend."

"And why on Earth should I care about your friend? Just another man taken out of society. Doesn't sound so bad to me," the woman said. "I wouldn't be surprised if your lady here feels the same. Darling, how often have you been at the mercy of whatever this man wants of you—especially now, with civilization lost?"

The woman turned toward Alayna. Alayna didn't speak. The woman laughed softly, as if she didn't need a response to know the truth. Clay was too distracted to comprehend the anxious spinning of Alayna's own mind.

"It's not just another man," Clay protested. "It's a boy. A teenage kid. He's going to die if we don't get him that medicine." He pointed at the backpacks "And the kid. He knows things. Things that could—"

The woman smiled grimly. "A boy, huh?" Her words dripped sarcasm. "Well. That changes everything."

Clay took a step forward. The woman's henchmen aimed their guns directly at Clay's heart.

"Please."

"I don't owe you anything," the woman snapped. "I don't owe you or this sniffling boy a goddamned thing. It's a dog eat dog world out here, to use an old expression." She turned, the heel of her boot crunching on the bloodstained glass. "You should just be grateful I saved your asses."

Clay was flabbergasted. He realized he hadn't faced another group of humans since riding into Helen. He hadn't expected such ruthlessness.

What had happened to this woman to make her this way? So bitter?

She began to walk away.

Alayna balled her hands into fists. "Wait!" she cried.

The woman's back stiffened.

"Wait," Alayna continued. "I'm asking for just an ounce of compassion. Just a little understanding, please. We're begging here."

The woman flipped her hair off her face, with a mannerism reminiscent of another time. When flirtatious actions spoke louder than words. The men on either side turned with her, prepared to aerate Alayna. But the woman held up a slim hand, staying them.

"Oh, honey," she said, her sarcastic tone unchanged. "If I give the two of you weapons, then you'll undoubtedly shoot us in the back. Imagine it from my side, won't you? Offer sympathy and understanding? Not today, dearie."

"We wouldn't do that," Clay stated. "Absolutely impossible."

"And what makes you say that?" Disbelief in her voice.

"I'm Clay Dobbs. That's why," he said. "I'm the sheriff of Carterville. This is Alayna Cordell, and she's my deputy. We're sworn to serve and protect, and we definitely wouldn't shoot you in the back. Not like cowards."

The woman looked surprised. Clay hoped he'd gotten through to her. She blinked several times. "My, my," she breathed. "If it isn't the sheriff of Carterville."

"Exactly." His heart started pumping again. "I knew you'd understand."

She cut him off. "That is to say—you *were* the sheriff of Carterville."

Clay's eyebrows furrowed. "What—"

"You *were* the sheriff. Just another servant to another dumpy little town that no longer exists. That is, if Carter-son-ville, or whatever it is, is anything like the other towns I've seen so far, it's nothing but a wasteland."

Thousands of images of Carterville flashed through Clay's mind. All the unique places that every town had that made it home. Memories that shaped him into the man he was today.

Could it really all be gone for good?

"If anything," the woman continued, "If anything, I should be worried about you and your deputy even more." The word "deputy" in air quotes, belittling them. "You've made it this long, in this . . . this nothingness. You've survived against these horrible creatures. You've had these weapons, and I'd bet that you haven't been afraid of using them. Otherwise, you'd be dead. Like the rest of the world. No, no. I think I'll keep all the weapons to myself. If you're worth anything, I think you'll be able to survive without them. And if not, that's not really my problem. Is it?"

She turned away, whispering curtly toward her soldiers. They began to retreat, easing through the mounds of death.

"Please," Clay said, his voice low. "We just need the medication. The kid at the hotel. The one who's sick—"

"I've already told you," the woman snapped. "I don't give a damn about your sick kid. I don't have time for it. This world doesn't have a future. Why should we give up anything to save him?"

"He knows things about my daughter," Clay said, spelling out his last hope. "He knows where she is, and that's all I care about anymore. I don't care about hurting you, or anyone else for the matter. You can go kill anyone you please. You can rule this dystopian universe, for all I care. I just want to find my daughter. My wife. My family."

42.

The woman stopped. Something in Clay's words reached her. She tilted her head slightly, almost birdlike, before turning to face them. She no longer wore that look of superiority—the one that implied she'd fill both Clay and his deputy full of bullet holes if they said another word about compassion or her lack of it.

Her new expression told a story, maybe of a past life—one rich in the matters of family, of love.

She stood there, silence stretching between them. Her comrades flicked their eyes from Alayna to Clay and back to Alayna, uncertain which one to point their guns at with the most ferocity.

Finally, when Clay thought that the reticence would go on forever, the blonde woman found her response. Her words were hesitant, reminiscent of someone who'd perhaps had lower self-esteem in the time before.

"How do I know you're not making them up? Your wife and daughter?" she asked. "As far as I know, you'd say just about anything to get what you want."

Clay shrugged, sensing a crack in her outer shell. "You really don't," he said truthfully. "I could tell you for five minutes the way Maia likes her oatmeal, or the way Valerie twirls her hair when she's nervous—but you're right, I could be making any of that up. You just have to take my word that I'm telling you the truth. I took an oath as a sheriff about a million years ago, pledging to be a truth seeker. Pledging to fight for justice."

"Justice," the woman echoed, her eyes fixed on Clay's. "I haven't heard that word in a long time. It doesn't seem to belong to this reality."

"My wife and daughter left Carterville before I did, right after the outbreak," Clay said, trying to start a dialogue. "I thought they'd be able to stay together, but apparently, they were separated when they got to Helen. My wife was sent to a military base up north, and my daughter—well. She was sent south. That's why I'm here."

"You're preaching to the choir," the woman said, her voice dropping.

"We found a boy at the nearby hotel. Like I said, he's very sick. But if we get him this medication, then he'll be able to tell us where they took her—my daughter. She apparently stayed with these people at the hotel. You understand? Once we get him to wake up, he can tell me where to go next. He's the missing link."

Beside him, Alayna flinched slightly. Clay's lie was subtle—giving a bit more weight to Alex's knowledge. All he'd said was Maia's name. That was true. That was going to have to be enough.

The seconds ticked away, a countdown approaching zero.

"Suppose I believe you," she started. "Suppose I believe everything, down to Maia eating oatmeal." Her eyes flashed. "What's in it for me, if I help you?"

Clay's mind raced. "If you do this, and I'm lying,

you can keep everything. You can keep our weapons. You can keep the medication. You can have all the supplies back at the hotel, even. But if we're telling the truth, we split everything equally. Except for the defibrillators. We get to keep those."

The woman glanced at the backpack filled with clunky devices. "And what on Earth is so important about those?" she asked. "Are you planning on having some sort of cardiac event?"

Clay offered her a small smile. Jokes were rare enough, especially coming from an enemy.

"We have—" he considered how much of his hand he should really show. "We have this device that actually neutralizes the crazed, without firing a single shot. But it needs a power source."

43.

The armed man on the left spoke up in a voice reminiscent of a cartoon villain.

"We shouldn't believe him, Sam," the man said. "They're lying. They obviously want to ambush us. And there's no telling how many of them there really are. We can't give them the upper hand."

Sam. That was the woman's name. Clay took it in, beginning to humanize her—if only slightly. He focused entirely on her as she began to shake her head, having already made up her mind.

"No," she said. "I don't think so. I'm a pretty good judge of character, as you know." With this, she rolled her eyes slightly—almost mocking herself.

The men beside her shifted, their boots crunching on the glass.

"I believe them," Sam said. "Clay Dobbs, Sheriff of Carterville. I think you've piqued my interest. I'll follow you to the hotel. If what you say is true, I get half of everything. Absolutely everything. That said—" she paused, giving weight to her next words. "I keep the defibrillators."

Clay's mind flashed on the two other defibrillators still on the shelf in the storage room. He nodded slowly, knowing he could come back and retrieve them whenever he pleased—if he got out of this alive. Focus on survival, he thought. "Sure. Okay. We have a deal."

But Alayna chose this moment to protest. "What do you need them for?" she asked, her voice tinged with anger. "We've already told you why we need them. We need them desperately." Tears began to glisten in her eyes.

Had she forgotten the other defibrillators, or was she just making a scene? Clay wondered, shifting uncomfortably.

Sam tilted her head back, reclaiming her authority with Alayna's protest. "You want them. You want them *desperately*. And so, my darling deputy, I want them too. And that's the end of it." She turned back to Clay. "Let's go."

She spun back, marching through the dead and leading them to five large trucks with their engines still purring. There, Clay and Alayna met her team of a dozen or so men, women, and children—each looking haggard, yet resolute. They all remained silent, and only stared.

"People," Sam addressed them. "We've met Clay and Alayna from Carterville, and we've negotiated a deal that could be quite good for all of us. We will follow them back to their hotel on the other side of town."

Taking a step forward, Clay addressed Sam. "It's going to be nearly impossible to drive there," he said. "The streets are full of abandoned vehicles. If you try to drive, it's going to take you all day to find a route. We came here on foot."

Sam's lips parted in a moment of shock. "Y-you walked here?" she asked, incredulous. "You're braver than I thought. Or maybe just crazy." She turned back to her crew. Her gun hung across her back, glinting. "Okay. We'll walk, while the rest of you drive as best as you can toward the hotel."

"You know where it is?" Clay began. "It's across town. Directly east of—"

Sam waved her hand. "We know this town," she said. "We've been through Dearing before. Isn't that right, people?"

Nobody in Sam's group offered a nod, or uttered a single sound. They seemed like shells of the humans they used to be, following Sam blindly, with nowhere else to turn.

"I'll get word to you from the hotel once the coast is clear," Sam said with finality.

Get word? Clay wondered. He'd long since discarded his cell phone once they'd discovered that the satellite network was no longer in operation. Was she planning to send up smoke signals?

Sam turned toward a darker man that was puffing a hand rolled cigarette, as if he were watching them all from far away. "Rodney. He says there's a sick kid at the hotel. Says it's a matter of life and death. You mind coming along?"

Rodney shrugged. He dropped from the back of the truck, still puffing. "I'll grab my medical bag."

Sam's eyes twinkled at Clay, she knew she looked impressive. "We have a doctor amongst us," she said. "How fortuitous for you. If you're telling the truth, that is."

44.

C lay and Alayna began to lead Sam and her small entourage toward the hotel. As they retraced their steps, the quaint southwestern town looked different. It still had an aura of gloom that seemed to blanket everything. But in the early morning hours, the rising sun cast an eerie glow on the vacant streets. Everyone remained alert, watching for the crazed in the shadows behind cars and between buildings. Clay and Alayna walked with their fists clenched as if they were weapons. They both felt naked, as good as dead unarmed.

Ten minutes into the hike, Alayna spoke up. "I'd feel much safer if I had my weapon. If they jump out in front of us. I'm doomed. And wouldn't we all be better off if—"

Sam cackled, interrupting Alayna's almost certainly rehearsed speech. "Don't worry your pretty face, darling," she said. "My boys and I will protect you. You saw it yourself. I've kept more than a dozen people alive since this all started. I can't be all bad at this game."

Alayna glared at Clay. He shrugged, trying to tell her, "It's going to be fine. We just have to get through this hard part, and then we'll get rid of these people."

There was so much he wanted to say, but he

knew he had to keep things to himself. Everything hinged on this. His daughter's life was at stake. He decided not to react to Alayna, as it only fueled her anger. There was nothing stopping Sam or her goons from murdering them in cold blood. Bleeding out on the streets of Dearing wasn't exactly one of Clay's preferences.

They walked in silence. Awkward glances from untrusting eyes in all directions. After many years as sheriff of Carterville, Clay had learned how to deal with just about every type of personality; he had to in order to get information from those that refused to give it . . . initially. As the minutes ticked by, he racked his brain, trying to come up with a way to get information out of Sam—a woman that was clearly resistant. After several minutes though, Sam broke the silence herself.

"So. It all began for you back in Carterville?"

"Yes," he said. How much should he tell her? He didn't know. Revealing that the outbreak had actually begun in Carterville, before spreading out to other parts of the world, seemed a bit much. "Some of us who stayed behind after the initial groups left Carterville made it to Helen a few weeks later."

There was so much he left out of that. The energy field. The lab. Leland. The military operation. The ones they'd left behind, dead.

"I see," Sam said. "And in Helen? What did you find there?"

"More of the same. We stayed there for a few days. Discussed what had gone down there in Helen with a few of the remaining survivors. They explained the evac process: who went north and who went south. Val, my wife, had been sent to Earlton. Since my daughter had shown signs of the illness, I knew she'd come this way."

"That's a Sophie's choice if I ever heard one," Sam said. "Choosing between your wife and your daughter."

"My wife's not ill," Clay said, his heart thumping. "I know she can take care of herself."

Even as he said it, he didn't truly believe it. Valerie's face flashed through his mind, becoming younger in his memory with each passing day. Now, he remembered her as a twenty-something, pregnant with Maia, anticipating the day that their family would start. Painting walls. Choosing decorations. Crying over drapes that had come in the mail in the wrong color.

Sam seemed uninterested. She proceeded to her next questions, stamping through Clay's uneasiness. "And the ones with the disease? How have you found them?"

"We had to learn to fight them," Clay said. "But since those first weeks, they seem to be adapting. Getting stronger. Recognizing our sounds, rather than just hunting us on sight alone. If we didn't have weapons . . ."

"We'd be dead," Alayna said, illustrating the point.

Sam didn't appear to notice. "What was it you said about your daughter being sent south? Because she was ill?"

Clay didn't answer immediately. He could feel his blood begin to boil at the mere thought of the atrocities committed by Wallace. "Ahh. The work of an insane—and I don't use that term loosely—Colonel Wallace. After he evac'ed Carterville, he wasn't happy. He continued on to flaunt his egotism in Helen, where I'm told that he rounded up some of the crazed and shipped them south. In big trucks," Clay said. "I don't know exactly where they went, though."

Sam didn't break stride, but she caught her breath, revealing that she was startled.

"So that Colonel's the piece of shit who sent them to me."

Clay spun to look at her, visibly shocked. "You know about the trucks?"

"I do," Sam said. "I was on duty one night. A dozen or so containers came into my shipping yard. Hordes of these monsters—it seemed like thousands of them, of people who were no longer people, you know—came pouring out of the containers. It was a complete horror show. Blood everywhere. All my men down there . . ."

"So, you fought them firsthand early on, then," Clay said.

"No. I was in the observation tower. I had to watch it all, like some kind of film. If I hadn't been up there, I'd be dead right now. Everyone else . . ."

"We've all lost a lot of people," Clay said, not sure that was any consolation.

Sam glossed over her moment of emotion. "Well, thankfully, they cleared out pretty quickly. Went on to ravage one town or the next, who knows. I was able to hide until I could calm down enough to think of what to do. Course, that feels like a forever ago, now. If I could only . . ."

Clay and Alayna didn't speak for a long time. They watched Rodney roll another cigarette, looking vaguely European. Clay remembered that his doctor had handed out anti-smoking pamphlets every time he'd gone in for a checkup, which never seemed frequent enough at the time. When had this doctor decided that enough was enough—that being dead sooner rather than later was preferable?

Maybe he had nothing left to live for. But what was with Sam? Was she living for the pure power? She seemed high on it, wielding a gun as if it were as natural to her as wearing a wristwatch. Imagining her quivering at the top of an observation tower, watching as her friends were mauled helped him understand who she could have been in the before. But how had she gotten to this after?

45.

"And the rest of you, how did you all come to . . . survive together?"

Sam seemed to weigh the price of telling the truth, of telling too much, much like Clay had earlier. "After I left the yard, I wasn't sure where to go. I didn't want to run into those same monsters on the road. It was pretty early in the morning. Nobody was awake, meaning they were safe in their beds. Behind locked doors. I drove as fast as I could back to my house, packed up some things, then called the people I knew—as many as I could. Told them to get to high ground. Told them to get ready. Rodney, he was my best friend's husband. Claire. But Claire—she was ..."

"Taken?" Clay finished.

"Killed," Rodney said, spitting his words through a cloud of smoke. "Told you to stop dwelling on it, Sam. Gotta fuckin' move on."

Sam didn't speak. It was clear she was embarrassed, but she ignored Rodney.

"It doesn't matter," she said. "We're all still alive, at least for now."

"Right. That's the important thing." He felt himself closer to Sam—realizing she was as human as he was, just trying to protect the ones depending on her. "Carterville was where it all started," he said.

Alayna inhaled sharply, shocked at Clay's statement.

Sam eyed him. "What do you mean?"

"It was a lab experiment. A Department of Defense project, using nanite technology to make human soldiers stronger, faster. But one of the scientists was a bit too clumsy with the experiments and released nanites into the town. God, it was a nightmare. Nobody knew what was going on. And it spread rapidly. We had to get the people out of there. What I didn't know at the time was that the mayor was actually aware of the entire project. She knew she was endangering the people of Carterville by allowing this lab."

"Shit," Sam replied. She continued her steady pace, but her shoulders loosened. "That must have been horrible. You were literally on the front line from day one. What happened to the project? I mean the research lab. Were you able to shut it down?"

"There were others," Clay said. "At least two that we know of. And that's what led us to Helen. We met up with two other scientists there. They'd been hiding out underground. One of them is with us now. At the hotel with the boy."

"And where did the others go?"

"They headed north, to the other military base. The one my wife is at," Clay said. "They took another one of the devices that I was telling you about. The ones that can wipe out the crazed with a single shot."

"And it really works?" Sam asked, sounding doubtful.

"It does," Clay said, nodding. "We used it on the way to the hotel. Wiped out a hundred of them. They just fell to the ground. Dead. No blood. No puss—no fuss. It was clean. And then it was over."

"Wow," Sam breathed.

Silence stretched between them once again. Sam's gunmen from the hospital—Clay had learned their names were Damon and Al, remained quiet throughout their journey—but it was Sam and Clay that settled into their own quiet contemplation, processing the information that they'd shared. Clay felt he'd found a new ally, someone with a mentality similar to his own. Even without the nanites pumping through her veins, Sam seemed strong, invulnerable, ready to walk a hundred miles without breaking a sweat.

"And what about this kid?" Sam said, breaking the silence.

"This boy. He's the next step," Clay said.

"What's he got?" she asked.

"I'm no doctor," Clay said. "But some kind of flu. He was left to die with it. Guess whoever he was with didn't have the presence of mind to see if he was going to turn or not."

"I can't say I blame them," Sam said. "If you started sniffling right now, I'd probably have them shoot you dead," she said nodding at Damon and Al.

"Ha." He kept to himself the information that he had already been exposed to the nanites. As he eased between two cars, he looked at Sam. "As soon as we get him better, he can tell me about my daughter."

"And he knows where they went?" Sam asked.

Without thinking, Clay responded, "I'm not sure. Right before he passed out, he said my daughter's name. That's what I'm going on right now. I'm sure once he's awake—"

Sam stopped in her tracks. Her gunmen followed suit, their steely eyes fixed on Clay. Clay's face clouded with confusion. Alayna stared at the ground, seeming to sense that the game was over.

"You lied to me," Sam said. "I can't believe this. You just walked into your own lie."

Clay raised his hands, his brain searching for what he'd lied about. "I'm sorry, what?"

"You said he knew where she was," Sam said in a huff. "You said the kid definitely knew where your daughter was, and that the moment he woke up, you'd know the truth. You said—"

"I pray that he knows where she is," Clay said, speaking over her.

Sam pointed her gun directly at Clay's face, her voice ragged. "No. You don't interrupt me, Sheriff Clay," she said. "In this world, I'm the sheriff. And you're just a liar."

"You're going to shoot me? Great," Clay said. "That means a kid back at the hotel will die because of you. That means my daughter will die. Because of you. That'll be on your shoulders, on your conscience. The meaningless deaths you would cause, Sam."

"This world doesn't hold a lot of meaning, anyway. It seems like I'd be saving you a lot of heartache. That kid could tell you your daughter's dead the moment he wakes up. Ever think of that?" Sam snarled.

The words sliced through him like a knife. With her gun pointed at him, he prepared for the worst, wanting to take a bullet like a man—wanting to feel every moment of his death.

But as they stared each other down, they heard a dramatic, screeching howl reverberate from a nearby alleyway—bouncing from brick to brick. It was time.

46.

Alayna whipped her head toward the sound, pulling her fists to her face. Damon and Al scanned the darkness in the alleyway. Before they could react, six of the monsters bounded from the alley, surrounding them.

Instinctively, Sam unslung her rifle but it fell from her hands. She lurched back against a vehicle, her eyes glazed with panic. Doc Rodney's cigarette dangled from his mouth, giving him a lost look.

The crazed were upon them. Clay screeched to Sam, "GET YOUR RIFLE, YOU IDIOT!"

Sam stumbled to the ground, feeling for it blindly, keeping her eyes on the advancing monsters. Once her hands found the weapon, she swung it up and started firing at the crazed. But her shots were wild, unable to aim from her position. Clay reached for his own gun, finding just an empty holster. Damon and Al leveled their guns as several of the crazed were pushed back by Sam's bullets. But the retreat was short lived. The crazed continued clambering at them.

"Aim for their heads!" Clay yelled, ducking behind a car and pulling Alayna out of the crossfire.

"All right, all right!" Sam cried, sounding frustrated. She fired at one, then another, splattering brain matter everywhere. Rejuvenated, she stepped forward to aim for another one, much further away.

"Fuck. Fuck," Alayna gasped behind him, gripping Clay's his bicep tightly.

Rodney hunched down, near the alleyway. Out of the corner of Clay's eye, he watched as one of the crazed lurch toward the doctor, ready to pounce on him. He cowered, his palms stretched skyward, braced against death.

Every cell in Clay's body screamed. He leaped to his feet and charged between the crazed and the doctor, facing the monster with only his fists. He heard Sam fire her gun at one of the crazed in the distance, leaving just him to help the doctor.

The monster snarled maniacally. Spit drooled from his mouth through rotting teeth. Bits of human flesh were caught in his teeth. His skin sagged showing its skeletal structure underneath. Clay shivered. Steeling himself, he delivered a heavy blow to the crazed's head, feeling the skull give slightly. It just inflamed the monster. He leaped at Clay, snarling, and pushed him to the ground. Clay fought like a tiger, using nails and feet to lash out at his attacker.

As the crazed's mouth came closer to Clay's throat, Clay caught the sides of the monster's mouth, ensuring he couldn't bite down. As if summoning a deeper strength, Clay howled in unison with the screech of the crazed, creating a strange cacophony in the abandoned town.

Sam danced around with her gun, trying to get a clear shot at the monster's skull. But the two were thrashing so wildly, she didn't dare shoot. Alayna stood beside her, helpless and tense, ready to spring into action.

The brawl continued. Clay seemed to get stronger as it dragged on. His biceps strained, his nails ripped into the papery skin of the crazed, streams of puss gushed out, splashing over Clay's clothing. The monster snarled and fought harder. Clay wished he had his gun, but—

"FUCK YOU!" Clay cried out, feeling that muscle fatigue was inevitable, and mere moments away. He had to make a move, and now.

Clay yanked the monster's mouth with both hands, and felt the jaw rip loose from the skull. The crazed howled as Clay tore it off completely, leaving only the rotted top teeth. Blood gushed from the monster's face onto Clay.

The monster rose and began to thrash more violently, bobbing his head, attempting to bite. He no longer depicted any form of human kind. Blood continued to pour from his face like a waterfall.

Clay jumped away, still holding the jaw. He pointed at the crazed. "Shoot! Shoot it now!".

Sam did as she was told. The bullet blasted through the crazed's brain. Immediately, its arms dropped as it stopped thrashing a crater in what was left of his head. A moment later, the crazed's legs buckled and it fell to the ground.

In the stillness that followed, Clay realized he was still holding onto the jawbone. He looked at it, eyeing the rotted, green teeth. With his nostrils flared, he realized he hadn't breathed in several moments. He took a breath and tossed the bloody jawbone to the ground.

47.

Silence followed as everyone stared at Clay. He was covered with blood and puss from the crazed, and bleeding from gashes of his own, on his arms and one across his eyebrow. He rubbed his sleeve across his cheeks and forehead, removing at least some of the blight from his beard. His heart still beat rapidly against his ribcage.

"Jesus, Clay." Alayna inched forward. "Are you all right?"

"We need to get moving." Clay turned back toward the hotel. "If we stay too long, more might come. Remember, they can hear us now. They can hunt."

"But Clay. Look at yourself—" Alayna protested.

Clay ignored her. As he marched forward, the blood began to dry on his arms and legs. He could hear the others in the behind him, whispering.

"He just ripped the jaw off," Sam said. "Clean off. Teeth and everything. I mean. I've never seen anyone capable of that."

"Barehanded," Damon said, whistling. "What's that about?"

"I don't know quite what we're dealing with here, but we can't let him out of our sight now."

Alayna kept quiet. For this, Clay was grateful.

She was the only one of them who knew about the nanites, about Clay's increasing strength. But neither of them had expected anything like this.

The surge of anger and strength had been unlike anything he'd ever experienced. He'd been unable to control it. It had been a part of him—eliminating all other emotions and driving him to act. He'd felt inhuman.

And then the jaw was in his hands. That dripping skeletal bone with rotting teeth digging into his fingers.

The lack of control scared Clay the most. Was that the nanites winning against his own humanity? Maybe he would slowly but surely become one of them. In the midst of another burst of rage, he could dive over the line between human and crazed, never to be seen again.

He imagined Sam blasting a bullet through his brain as he tried to gnaw her throat.

Alayna crept up beside him as they marched. She nudged him with her elbow, whispering, "Are you all right? You didn't answer me back there. Talk to me, Sheriff. You can't leave me out on this."

Clay responded brightly, not wanting to worry her. "I'm fine, Alayna," he said. "I saw that the crazed was going to take the doctor, and I couldn't let it happen. I did what I could to help him. I know you would have done the same."

Alayna looked doubtful. She didn't believe him.

"If we'd only had weapons, none of that would have happened," Clay said, his voice low. He knew if he struck a chord with Alayna, she'd back off.

"Tell me about it," Alayna breathed. "The sooner we can have our guns back, the better. I'm seriously freaking out about it. I feel naked."

"You'd think after an attack like that, they would give them back," Clay whispered back, grateful that Alayna was dropping the issue. He didn't want to face it himself. "Anyway, we're just around the corner from the hotel. I think we'll make it without another fatality."

"Those sound like some last words," Alayna said, giving him a half grin.

Clay grimaced and cut his eyes back to the front, still reeling from the shock of his mountainous rage. He needed to regain control. He remembered what it had felt like to hold his daughter for the first time, when she'd been an infant. How small she'd been in his arms, how delicate. He'd looked down at her, conscious that his muscles were tense, trying to keep his body entirely still so as not to in any way rock her world.

He needed that kind of control over his body again. He needed to restrain his strength, to only use it when it was necessary. The entire world was just as delicate as baby Maia had been.

In any case, he knew he'd proven something to Sam and the others. But he wasn't entirely sure he'd proven something good.

48.

The hotel was quite the sight to see in full daylight. With the drama of the past twelve-plus hours, Clay had almost forgotten about the score of dead bodies on the hotel's front steps. The crazed were still piled atop one another, decomposing in the morning sun.

"Wow," Sam breathed, impressed, or slightly disturbed.

They stood behind the mound of corpses, looking up at the hotel entrance. Clay rested his hands on his waist, trying to ignore the dense stench.

"What happened here?" Sam asked, her voice almost light. "A sign of your handiwork, I take it? Course, I don't see the jaws separated from the bodies in this pile. A bit of laziness on your part, Clay."

Clay rolled his eyes, not giving her a response. But inwardly, he appreciated her attempt at humor. An hour before, she'd been ready to put a bullet through his head. Now, she was cracking jokes. Hopefully this was a sign that not all of humanity was lost.

At the very least, it meant she wasn't yet too frightened of him to be sarcastic.

Damon and Al entered the sea of dead first,

clearing a path toward the front door. The others followed, with Sam bringing up the rear, her rifle held tightly in her hands. Clay tried his best not to look at the dead, but not because he was worried that he'd recognize someone from his past, but because he was fearful of seeing more of himself in them.

They entered the hotel through the shattered glass door, compliments of Alayna's badassedness.

"Subtle," Sam said, joking again. "You didn't bother to try the door?"

"It must have been the adrenaline," Alayna said. "I got caught up in the moment. What's another glass door at the end of the world?"

Sam nodded. "Not gonna lie, we've done it too. Still, it's a shame that we'll never experience the good things in life again. So, why not take what we need?"

"The grocery stores are hard to explore," Alayna said. "All that rotting fruit. And the meat. It's a horrible smell."

"We've stuck to gas stations, mainly. Although living off of chips and pretzels isn't going to keep us going much longer," Sam said.

"Same," Clay said.

"So hungry," Alayna said, passing the concierge desk, her eyes drifting toward the kitchen.

"A constant state, isn't it?" Sam agreed. Her eyes turned to Clay. "So. You want to take us to the kid?"

Damon stepped closer to Clay, unslinging his rifle as if to say, "Make one false move, motherfucker."

"Sure thing," Clay said, and started for the staircase. "And in just a few minutes, you'll see that we've done nothing but tell you the truth."

"You've already lied. But it's your lucky day, I guess," Sam said from behind him. "I've decided forgiveness is the best route in your case. I really like my jaw where it is. Some ex-boyfriends said it was one of my best features."

Clay laughed, in spite of everything. With a last burst of energy, he bolted to the top of the steps, landing on the fourth floor hardly out of breath. Waiting for the others to catch up, he closed his eyes for a moment—praying inwardly that Alex was still alive. That he'd been able to rest. That Lane had found a way to keep him tethered to the world for a while longer.

Please, he thought. This is the last thing I'll ask for. I promise.

Who am I talking to? he wondered half-heartedly. Was anyone watching over them? Was there anyone to pray to? He'd never bothered much with church in the time before, opting to sleep in on Sundays instead. But the concept of a higher power had never been something he'd eliminated completely.

Please, he thought again, as Sam and Alayna landed beside him. Just this once.

"Down the hall," Clay said, taking long strides toward the furthest room. They followed behind him like ants in a line, with Sam directly behind Clay. When he reached it, he knocked sharply, and opened the door.

Immediately, Lane raised her gun, pointing it at the them. Her nostrils were flared, making her look almost demonic, like a bear watching over her cubs. For several seconds, Clay stood at the door with his hands high.

"Lane. It's me," Clay said softly. "Put the gun down."

Lane dropped her aim and flung herself across

the room, hugging Clay close. She shuddered. "You were gone so long, I didn't think you were coming back."

"It's all right," he said, looking at Alex who was barely breathing. He was still sweating, and he appeared to be talking in his sleep, mumbling incomprehensible words. "We brought some reinforcements. Meet Sam."

Sam nodded curtly. "The scientist?"

"That's right," Lane said, extending her hand.

As she stepped into the room, the stench from before—the soiled sheets, the clothing, reared its ugly head. Perhaps Lane had grown accustomed to it in the hours she'd sat there alone, spinning in her own head. Sam backed into the hallway, pointing at the sick child. "Rodney, I think this is your time to shine," she said, her voice still holding its sarcastic tone. "I can't stay in there another second. It smells like death warmed over. And God, am I tired of that smell."

49.

R odney dropped his cigarette in the hallway and extinguished it with the toe of his shoe, then approached Alex's bed. Clay watched him curiously. The man hadn't said much, making him more mysterious than he probably was. But he worked diligently, looking practiced in his bedside manner, lifting Alex's wrist slightly and checking his vitals.

Clay stood by the bed, Alayna next to him. Lane hunched near the door, looking almost ready to fall apart after having the room and Alex to herself for so long. The boy was even more sallow than he'd been, resembling the dead that piled up outside the hotel. His cheeks were so sunken they could hold pools.

"What's it look like, Doctor?" Clay asked, addressing Rodney properly.

The doctor didn't move. "He's malnourished, severely dehydrated," he said. "His pulse is quite weak. When was the last time you saw him conscious?"

"About twelve hours ago," Lane said.

Rodney motioned toward the backpacks, gesturing for them to bring the one with medications toward him. Alayna yanked it away from Al and handed it to him. Ripping open the zipper, the man began to sift through the various bottles of pills, reading the brand names and muttering to himself.

Sam whispered to one of her gunmen, eyeing the boy. Clay thought she was making a bet that the boy would die within the hour. Despite showing a bit of humanity earlier, he knew he couldn't trust someone like her. Someone who'd been willing to steal their guns and their medication, indifferent to them.

Finally, the doctor took three bottles from the backpack and shook them like rattles. "Found it," he said.

Alayna perked up. "Is he going to make it?"

"I don't know," Rodney said. He popped open the top of the first medication with a tight twist of his wrist. "I really don't. But what I do know is that I need privacy. Please." He gestured at the door. "Let me work on him in private. And good god, get those soiled linens out of here. They reek."

Clay nodded and went into the hallway. Alayna and Lane followed, but not before Lane scooped up Alex's stained sheets and clothes. The six of them formed a circle, looking like loiterers, lost, blinking at one another. Except for Alayna, Clay wouldn't have known any of these people in his real life. He wouldn't have gone out of his way to say good morning to them. He wouldn't have helped them with their groceries.

So he waited, knowing good and well that one of the women would certainly step up.

Lane fulfilled Clay's prophecy.

"Did you find the defibrillators?" she asked, resting her hand on Clay's forearm. She looked at him anxiously.

Sam grunted to herself, shifting her weight.

Clay looked at Sam, unsure of what to say.

Sam studied Clay for several seconds before

finally pulling a cell phone from her backpack. Her fingers danced across the display before she muttered into it: "All clear. Make your way to the hotel, but be on the lookout. Some of the monsters, or the crazed, as the sheriff calls them, are roaming the streets. I repeat. Some of the crazed have been spotted." Still, her eyes remained on Clay, questioning.

Clay was overwhelmed be several things just then. First, how in the hell did Sam's cell phone work, and second, what on Earth had he done to make her so suspicious?

Maybe ripping the jaw from the guy's skull. Maybe that had had something to do with it. Maybe.

Jesus.

"Well?" Lane pressed, waiting. "The defibrillators?"

Sam gestured for Damon. He passed the backpack with the defibrillators to Clay.

Clay nodded thanks, shocked that she'd given them over so readily. What had changed her mind?

"I hope your science thing works. I really do," Sam said, crossing her arms. "I'm really tired of seeing so much blood spilled. Quite tired of it, indeed."

Clay and Sam sized each other up, with suspicion on one side and gratitude on the other. Clay opened the backpack, eyeing the defibrillators within. Lane clapped her hands together excitedly, the sound reverberating in the corridor. Damon and Al remained stone faced, as if they were mere soldiers in a greater game—pawns to be played whenever Sam chose.

Clay, someone who was never great with words, was suddenly flooded with things to say. In the end, he decided to keep it simple. Keep it real.

"Thank you, Sam."

Sam searched his face, but only nodded in reply.

50.

Lane took the backpack and pulled out one of the defibrillators. She gasped at the heft of the device. "Yes," she said with glee. "You don't know just how much this will help us. Help you. Help the world," she said to Sam.

"Yeah, sure," Sam said, turning toward the staircase. "I think I need a fucking drink. There a bar in this place that hasn't been ransacked quite yet?"

Clay thought back to when they'd initially searched the hotel. There'd been a small bar attached to the auditorium that might have a few bottles of spirits left. "Downstairs. The dining room on the west side of the hotel. I think I saw a bar down there. I'm not sure what you'll find, but that's where I'd head first," he said.

Sam nodded curtly. "That might be the best news I've heard all day. Let's go. Damon. Al."

Clay watched them go, reminding himself to talk to her about their cell phone reception later. Lane scurried off with the defibrillators and ducked into another room, where she set up a makeshift lab while they'd been gone.

Alayna appeared beside him. She looked like she'd been crying. He touched her shoulder with his dirt-caked hand, suddenly conscious that he needed to clean himself up. She didn't appear to notice.

"Clay? I—I need to talk to you about something," she said softly.

Clay raised his eyebrows, wary. He remembered the "talk" he'd had with her a few days before, when he'd told her it simply couldn't happen between them. Not now. Not ever. Not with Valerie somewhere, waiting for him to save her. Would Alayna want to talk about it all over again?

"It's important," she insisted. "And I think you owe it to me to listen."

Clay nodded slowly, trying to read her face. But it revealed nothing.

"All right," Clay said, shrugging. "Let me just find someplace to get cleaned up first. Then let's see if we can find some coffee down in the kitchen. Something normal for both of us."

Alayna nodded silently.

With a heavy sigh, Clay ventured to another room, where he scrubbed his filthy hands in the passably clean toilet. He felt a slight twinge of disgust, but reminded himself of what he'd done earlier that day. Nothing about a toilet's water should disgust him any longer.

He rejoined Alayna in the hall, taking in her worried face.

When they got to the kitchen, he busied himself, bouncing from cabinet to cabinet, on the hunt for coffee grounds. Each cabinet seemed emptier than the last. He started to whistle, wanting to make Alayna feel more comfortable. She stood with her arms crossed, and her mind seemingly elsewhere, watching him search.

"Man, they really went through this place," Clay said. "I mean, I can't blame them. I would have done the same. Ah—wait." He opened up the last cabinet by the walk-in freezer and found a few packs of instant coffee hiding in the back of the cabinet, behind a half-eaten jar of moldy jelly. He lifted them triumphantly, hopeful this would give them a moment of normalcy.

"Now, I just need to make some hot water."

Alayna still didn't speak. Clay organized the coffee on the counter, almost manic in his movements. He was still bursting with unlimited energy.

"Clay. Clay. Hey. Can you please stop for a second?" Alayna asked. "I have something to tell you. Something serious."

Clay turned toward the cabinets again, hunting for a pan—anything to heat up the water. "Mmm?" he murmured. "I wonder what they would have done with all the pots and pans . . ."

"Clay. Seriously. Listen," Alayna said. Her face was pale with fright.

Clay closed the cabinet slowly. "All right," he said. "What is it you want to say?"

"I have it," Alayna whispered, her voice catching. "I have what you have. I think you infected me."

Thinking Alayna probably just had a cold, or was exhausted after so much traveling, Clay waved it off. "No, Alayna. That's impossible. I told you in the forest that if we made love, I'd infect you. But we haven't. Unless you took advantage of me while I was sleeping." He chortled, hoping to lighten her mood.

But Alayna didn't react.

"We made love in the hotel before we left Carterville, Clay. You remember? That actually happened, whether you want to remember it or not. And you were already infected by then. I think you infected me."

Waves of shock crashed over him as he realized she was right. How had he not put this together before? He stared at her, the coffee forgotten.

"Oh, God," Clay whispered. "You must be feeling . . . I mean, are you okay?"

"I don't know what I'm feeling," Alayna said. "It started when we were at the hospital. Or maybe when we got here and I found myself vomiting in the hallway. Either way, all the blood and gore is really getting to me. You know me, Clay. I normally have an iron stomach. And then when I saw you—" She paused, hunting for words. "When I saw you mutilate that crazed earlier, I almost lost it completely. I can't think of another explanation. I'm feeling ill just thinking about it."

Tears began to stream down her cheeks. Clay wrapped his arms around her shoulders, holding her close. He tried to make sense of it all. The first days of his symptoms—what had they been like? Similar? Yes. He'd been nauseous, achy, having to overcome the weakness of his stomach in order to keep track of his people.

But wouldn't Alayna have started having these symptoms weeks ago, after they'd made love? It didn't make any sense. But then again—nothing in this world made sense.

"We'll get through this," Clay said into her ear, trying to soothe her. "If you have it, we'll do everything we can to get it out of you. I mean that."

Alayna pushed away. "Don't lie like that, Clay," she said. "We can't even get this—this thing out of *you*. And you're changing so fast. I'm so scared."

Faced with the strength of Alayna's emotions, Clay couldn't deny his own fear anymore.

Shuddering, he pulled her closer. "I'm afraid, too," he said, speaking the truth for the first time. "I mean, when I ripped that monster's face off, I didn't know I was capable of something like that. It was horrible, Alayna. And wonderful at the same time."

Alayna wiped tears from her cheek.

"Tell you what," Clay said. "If either of us turns into one of the crazed, the other one promises to take care of things before taking care of themselves."

"Taking care?" Alayna turned the thought over in her mind. "I suppose you're right. It's the only way," she said to herself. "Murder, suicide. I never thought we'd be having *this* discussion."

Clay held her tight. "Me neither, Alayna. Me neither."

They stood there, lost in their own thoughts. Clay wanted to say more, but deep down, he knew that sometimes words were better left unsaid.

"Now that we've cleared up that incredibly, not awkward at all situation," Clay said, trying to lighten the mood, "Why don't we find a quiet room so you can get some rest? You look exhausted."

There were half-moon shadows beneath her eyes, blood flecks across her chin

"I would say the same for you," Alayna said. "Scientifically speaking, you should look as rough as me. We haven't slept in days. But you look more vibrant and alive than ever. Do you even feel tired at all?"

Clay straightened up, breaking the hug. He flexed his biceps, marveling at the strength that seemed to build, minute by minute. He could almost feel the muscle fibers joining together. "I feel fantastic," he said, the words almost incidental.

Alayna nodded. Nothing else needed to be said.

She turned back to the door of the kitchen, with Clay following behind. Their hearts were heavy at their disturbing realization. For a moment, Clay had the strangest desire to hold her hand. But he pushed the impulse back. No use complicating things.

51.

After putting Alayna to bed, Clay sat up for another hour or two, sitting in a chair by the window, staring at his hands—amazed at how strong he was becoming, and yet how powerless he remained. Checking that Alayna was still resting comfortably, he decided to return to his coffee mission. He wasn't fatigued enough to need a cup, but the feeling of that routine—of sipping a mug of hot bean water—might help bring his mind from the brink of insanity.

He needed a bit of normalcy. Even if only for a moment.

Once in the kitchen, he was able to fill the glass pot with water from a water cooler near the freezer door. Grateful that it wasn't toilet water, he guzzled a bit of it from the pot. As he wiped his mouth, he realized he had no mechanism by which to boil the sucker.

Shit.

He caught a glimpse of the outside through the window. Darkness was falling, thrusting them into another terrifying night in this strange town. He hated that they'd destroyed the glass door when they'd entered, putting them at the mercy of whatever crazed came upon them.

The kitchen door swung open. Sam walked in, alone, carrying his pistol and rifle. She passed them to him carefully, without a word. Clay slid the pistol back into his holster and set the rifle on the counter, next to the coffee. He nodded gratefully.

"I suppose I owe you an apology," she said, folding her arms across her chest. "After all that's happened, it's difficult to know who to trust. Apparently, I'm not that good a judge of character. It wasn't personal."

Clay considered her words, remembering how cold she'd been when she'd confronted them at the hospital. They lost so much time in the back and forth. And if she hadn't listened to him about his daughter, they'd be watching Alex die right now. He wasn't sure how much he could forgive her.

"I guess I wouldn't trust me either," Clay said, half-lying. "Considering the situation we're in."

He wanted to believe he wouldn't be as horrible as she had been. But of course, he couldn't be certain.

"So, what's your plan?" Sam asked, leaning against the counter and eyeing the half-filled pot.

"Certainly not heating the water, that's for sure," Clay said, giving her a half smile. Tipping his head toward the staircase, he continued, "When the kid's awake, I want to learn more about the people he was traveling with. I want to know where they might have taken Maia."

"And you think they have Maia?" Sam asked. "Why are you so sure?"

Clay hesitated, feeling her doubt pouring over him. "It's a gut feeling. Which I know, shouldn't amount to much. But if you had seen the way he was talking about Maia, you'd know there was something to it. More than just knowing her name. There was a connection between them. So much so that the moment before he nearly died, he said her name repeatedly. If that's all I have to go on, then so be it. I'll take it."

She considered his words carefully, but made no reply.

"And you?" Clay asked her. "Are you on your way somewhere?"

Sam shrugged. For the first time, the muscles in her face relaxed to reveal a layer of confusion and fear. "I'm not sure," she said. "My family's all gone. I have my people—the ones I cared enough about to call, and the stragglers I picked up on the way. But now we're just looking for a sanctuary. At the same time, I don't know what the rest of the world's like. I'm scared of staying in one place for too long. Getting comfortable somewhere. Calling it home? It doesn't sound possible in a world so cruel."

Clay remembered the moments of comfort he and the others had felt before: at the hotel in Carterville, back in Helen. Always, those feelings were tainted when they'd been pushed too far.

"I know what you mean," Clay said, noticing Sam's cell phone bulging in her hip pocket.

"Hey, I meant to ask about that," he said, gesturing to it. "How in the hell did you maintain cell phone reception? We lost connectivity more than a month ago."

Sam slipped the shiny black phone from her pocket and swiped across the screen, waking it from sleep mode. "You noticed that, huh? Dwayne, a guy we picked up along the way was able to reprogram all our phones to connect to one another, without the use of cell towers. He called it hawking, or something

. . ."

"Ad hoc? I've heard of it, but never realized it was actually possible."

Sam handed Clay the phone, and he tapped out Valerie's phone number and hit the send button.

Nothing happened.

"It doesn't actually work like that," she said. "It's more of just a walkie-talkie, and the distance is limited to other node's close by."

Clay's moment of anticipation faded quickly as he handed the phone back. "I suppose that it's still encouraging; not all we had is lost. If one stranger can put us all back into communication, humanity still might have a chance—"

Lane burst into the kitchen, panting. She looked at Clay as a smile stretched her face—one of pure, unadulterated joy.

"I've done it," she said, triumphantly. "I fixed it."

52.

"The neutralizer?" Clay asked, inhaling slightly.

"Yes," Lane said, rubbing her palms together. "It took a bit of adjustment inside the device itself. But I think the thing works. The battery interface wasn't perfect—not exactly the way we designed it. But I got it in there."

Sam and Clay exchanged a glance, Sam looked a bit confused. Despite her own bit of technological show and tell, this was far more advanced than the life she'd been living for the past month: kill or be killed, eat or be eaten.

"That's wonderful," Clay exclaimed.

Lane's eyes sparkled, making her look almost cocky. "Anyone care for a demonstration?" she asked, grinning madly.

"I've heard so much about this gizmo, I'd be up for a show," Sam replied.

Lane clapped her hands excitedly, and hurried back upstairs to fetch the device. Clay slung his rifle over his shoulder, excited to be armed once again, then he and Sam met Lane at the entrance, looking out at the dark streets. When their eyes adjusted, they crunched through the broken glass and then walked through the dead crazed, to the street. The stench of the decomposing crazed was horrific, making them hold their breath as they passed.

"Strange to be hunting for them, instead of the other way around," Clay whispered, once they were clear.

"As it's night, I don't think it'll take too long to find them," Sam said. "We've found that they're more active at night. At least that's what we experienced."

"Look," Lane said, pointing across the street. She pointed with the neutralizer. "I think I see one in the alley."

"Ah. Yeah," Sam said, leaning forward and drawing her gun. "Strange she's by herself. Kinda weird fighting the urge to take a shot at it right now. You're saying that thing can take it out instantly?"

"Well, not quite, but yeah," Lane said, sensing that Sam didn't trust the neutralizer. Her eyes gave away her reluctance to speak with Sam, this stranger.

"Looks like she's spotted us," Clay observed.

As if on cue, the crazed—a middle aged women wearing a dingy sundress and one high heel—scrambled out of the alley and came at them, a howl rising from deep in her throat. Her arms clawed at the air, ready to rip into them. Hair streamed down her back, curling slightly with the wind whipping in from the mountains.

Lane swung the device toward the monster, aiming it with precision.

"Any time, now," Sam whispered, her voice raspy. "Otherwise I'll take care of things . . ."

"All right, all right," Lane said, rolling her eyes. She squeezed the trigger with confidence, sending the invisible waves into the air.

But nothing happened. The crazed continued to ramble forward. Filled with rising panic, Clay aimed at the crazed, prepared to shoot.

"I don't understand," Lane said, sounding troubled. She turned it over searching for an explanation. The crazed was now a mere eight feet away, moving fast. One of them was about to be its food.

"Lane! I'm going to shoot!" Clay warned.

"Oh! Stupid me," Lane gasped. "I forgot to turn it on."

She flicked the power switch. A soft hum emanated from the interior, indicating it was fully charged. She squeezed the trigger again.

Four feet away, the crazed stopped in its tracks, staring at them quizzically. Its dried-out, purple-tinted lips remained open, exposing rotting teeth. Its skin sagged at the corners of its eyes as it stared ahead—perhaps realizing, for a mere second—that it'd once been human, and was now something else entirely.

It dropped to the ground, falling first to its knees and then to its face, shattering its nose and cheekbones. Sam remained standing with her gun drawn, still skeptical of what she'd just witnessed.

"Wow," she said, still prepared to shoot, as if she thought the crazed was playing dead. "That was . . . really something."

Lane grinned with pride. She held the neutralizer up, admiring her handiwork.

Behind them, Alayna's voice piped up, "Damn. That was close."

Clay jumped, startled. "Shit. Alayna. I didn't even hear you come out," he said.

"Are you trying to scare us to death?" Lane asked, her eyes wide.

Alayna chuckled. She looked a bit better after

her rest, although the bags were still prominent under her eyes.

"Haven't had the power to frighten anyone in a while," she said, smiling. "A bit refreshing, really. Anyway. Doc Rodney wanted me to tell you that Alex just woke up."

Clay's heart began to hammer. Incredibly, he'd forgotten about the boy. "Can he speak?"

"He can," Alayna said. "He's ready for you."

Clay sprinted to the hotel entrance, oblivious to the others behind him, focused wholly on the upcoming conversation. Whatever Alex told him would alter the course of his life. Information that he would have to accept.

Even if Alex told him something he wasn't prepared to hear.

53.

W hen Clay entered Alex's room, he felt oddly manic. Blood pumped against his eardrums, making it difficult to hear anything but his own breathing. Dropping his gun at the door, he went to the bed, where he found Rodney seated beside the skeletal boy, feeding him something sour-smelling that looked like applesauce.

With Clay's arrival, both Alex and Rodney looked up expectantly. The boy was chewing slowly, taking in every bit of energy. His eyes were orbs, too bright and too big for what remained of his skinny frame. Lane, Sam, and Alayna entered a minute later, having fallen behind Clay in his race from the ground floor. After caring for boy for so long, Lane reached for his hand and squeezed it gently.

"How are you feeling?" she asked, her voice colored with sadness.

Alex gave her a small smile. There was no way he remembered her. Maybe he trusted something in her face. "Much better, thank you," he said softly.

Clay's heart squeezed. He dropped to his knees beside the bed, amazed at the transformation the kid had made since they'd found him. "Rodney, this is really something," he whispered. "He's completely—"

"He still has a long way to go before he's healthy,"

Rodney said, leaning back. The boy lifted his other hand and took the bowl of applesauce, starting to scrape it clean. "But get a lot more food in him, and he'll regain his strength in no time."

"Alex. Right? That's your name?" Clay asked him.

The kid nodded. "Yeah. That's it. Do I know you?"

"You were pretty out of it when we found you," Clay said.

"The fever dreams I had were wild. Strange ones. About zombies? And about a million other things. Aliens coming to earth. Getting a D on my math test."

Behind Clay, Alayna chortled softly at the joke. Sam shifted uncomfortably, clearly uncertain if she should care about every aspect of the kid or get straight to the point. Clay focused on Alex, ready to dig for information.

"So, what's the last real thing you remember?" he asked.

"The last memory." Alex looked thoughtful. "It's pretty harsh. I remember Malcolm, of course. He was tying me to this bed. Everything seemed blurry, though, so I can't remember what he said before . . . But the ropes—around my wrists—and then the door clicking as he went away and left me. I remember that." Alex's words were still jumbled, but the gist of it came through clearly.

"Malcolm?" Clay asked. "Who's Malcolm?"

Behind him, Sam gasped. Clay glanced at her, seeing her jaw drop. But he returned his attention to Alex.

"Malcolm is—was our leader. The group I was in for a while, at least. There were about thirty of us, give or take, mostly men but a few women," he said. He dropped his bowl and put his hands across his chest. His cheeks already seemed fuller.

"And you were traveling together?" Clay asked.

"Going from town to town around here. Hunting for supplies. We came to the hotel and God—that was a sight to see," Alex replied.

"How so?" Clay asked. He still hadn't mentioned Maia. When was he going to get to Maia?

"When we got here, half the rooms were filled with those things. Locked inside, you know. Trying to get out. Malcolm decided to check on all of them to see if anyone had survived. It seemed like some kind of weird science experiment. Like a bunch of rats in a cage," Alex said. "But there were some who'd survived. Who weren't monsters yet. Maybe eight or nine? I lost count."

Clay's heart leaped. "Was one of them named Maia?"

"What about a Megan?" Alayna asked, leaping over Clay's words. "Was there a survivor named Megan?"

Alex shook his head sadly, his eyes glassy. "I don't remember all of them. I wish I could, but everything was confusing. I was starting to get sick and was out of it most of the time. But there was a girl. A girl around my age, or a bit younger. She was really sick. We talked a lot. I tried to help her. She was—she was the nicest person I'd met in a long time."

Clay bowed his head, praying. "Do you remember her name?" he asked patiently, but struggling with frustration inside.

Alex nodded. "Maia, I think. That's right. That was her name."

"And she left with the others?" Clay demanded, almost insane with worry.

"I wasn't the only one who liked her. When she started to get a better, Malcolm really took notice of her," Alex said, his eyes turning toward the window. He swallowed hard, clearly losing steam. "He took her. He chained her up. They left with her."

Clay stared into Alex's face. "Chained her?"

"Like some kind of animal," Alex said, his eyes moistening. "It was horrible. Malcolm wouldn't listen to me. I was getting too sick, anyway—"

"He wouldn't listen to you, despite being your father?" Sam asked from behind Clay, staring down at Alex with eagle eyes.

Clay and Alayna gaped at Sam, wondering how in the world she'd known that. Alex began to nod; his breathing grew shallow.

"How did you know that?" he asked her. "I haven't called him my father for a long, long time."

Clay's blood felt close to boiling. He imagined Maia, chained to this horrible man, being dragged through town, her small feet trying to keep up with him. "Your father. He chained Maia up?" He was barely able to get the words out as his agitation swelled. Bolting to his feet, he glared down at Alex— the current source of his anxiety. "He chained up my daughter. And he carted her away like an animal?"

Alayna moved forward, placing a hand on Clay's shoulder. She rubbed at the tense muscle, trying to soothe him. "Shhh," she whispered. "We're going to find her."

But Clay shrugged her off with a violent motion. He barreled from the room, so enraged he could barely see.

The world was crumbling around him.

54.

O nce in the hallway, Clay let go. Agitation and rage ripped through him, causing him to batter the walls, to punch holes in doors. He was in a mode of destruction, leaving debris in his wake. Tears streamed down his face. His cheeks burned. "FUCK!" he screamed, beating his knuckles against the staircase walls, feeling the plaster crumble under his fists. Nothing could fight back; he could tear the entire hotel down, if he wanted.

And in that moment, he wanted something to feel as badly as he did. To look as ruined as he felt.

The others followed, watching as he ripped and tore at the bones of the hotel itself, shattering windows and allowing blood to course down his arms and legs. His heart felt like it might burst from the inside out and splatter against the floors below. He couldn't feel anything else.

In the lobby, Clay flattened his palms against the reception desk. He remembered feeling as if his daughter had been in the hotel from the very moment they'd walked in. He'd felt her presence there; he'd sensed that she'd been a part of whatever had happened, whatever made it such a horrible, grey, shadowed environment.

She'd been locked in a hotel room, while the rest

of the travelers she'd come with from Helen had turned into the crazed all around her.

How she'd survived that long was beyond Clay.

He screamed again, a frightening howl from deep within his chest, then he tore the top of the reception desk off, hoisting the massive granite slab above his head. Phone cables and power cords dangled to the floor. Holding it aloft, he caught a glimpse of Alayna out of the corner of his eyes, sobbing uncontrollably at his complete and utter breakdown. With a flourish, Clay hurled the counter at the wide open front door, and into the darkness outside. The granite shattered on the noses and skulls of the crazed, creating a noise almost too horrible to imagine. Alayna covered her mouth, surely about to vomit again.

In the silence afterward, Clay collapsed against the wall, covering his face with his hands. He began to sob, adding to Alayna's wails, unable to process the truth of what Alex had told him. He'd wanted to be strong, for Maia. He'd wanted to accept the truth. But faced with it, he recognized how truly powerless he was.

Alayna went to him then. She knelt down beside him, lifting his bloodied hand to her lips. She kissed it, watching as his face changed.

"They have her. They have my Maia," he whispered, his voice raspy.

"I know. I'm so sorry, Clay. I'm so—"

"I have to get her back, Alayna. I have to fight."

"And we will," Alayna's words were sure. "After you left, Alex said they were more than likely headed back to their compound."

Clay sat up, his attention on Alayna's words. His heartbeat began to slow as he began to understand their meaning.

"It's a bit north of here. In the woods. You know, I was thinking about our walk here. That dirt road, where they took the Jeep. I wouldn't be surprised if it's up there. Otherwise, we would have seen the compound," Alayna said.

"You really think it was Malcolm?" Clay asked, dubious.

"I heard his name," Alayna said. "When they were stealing it. I heard someone call for a Malcolm to check it out."

"So, he had Maia with him when he took the Jeep?" Clay gasped. "Could it be? I mean how many other groups of survivors are there?"

Alayna shrugged, looking unsure. "I don't know. But Alex is willing to lead us to the compound. As soon as he's well."

"And he's okay with turning on his father?" Clay asked, skeptical.

The others came closer, listening. Sam clutched her gun, her eyes fixed on the open door, almost certain they'd be under attack at any moment.

"I don't get the feeling that Alex cares much for his father anymore," Alayna said, glancing back at Sam. "And Sam mentioned that she's had dealings with him in the past, as well. He's apparently psychotic, to put it mildly. She wouldn't go into too many details, though."

Clay's eyebrow twitched. What was the story there? Sam had begun to pace the edge of the room, her gun drawn, clearly deep in thought. He would approach her with this issue later.

"Doc Rodney says Alex can travel in a few days. So, there's that. Finally, something to look forward to," Alayna said, brushing plaster specks from Clay's growing beard. "Sheriff. When was the last time you slept?"

"Ha. Sleeping is for the weak," Clay said sarcastically, turning his eyes to his bloodied hands. He could no longer remember all the damage he'd caused, but could see the shattered glass embedded in his skin. God, he really was turning into a monster.

"Did you even sleep that night in the forest?" Alayna asked.

"No. I can't remember. I've been awake, just making sure we're all okay. Making sure nobody came at us," Clay said.

"Well, that won't do. You're still human enough. You need your sleep," Alayna said, rising, and taking Clay's hand. With a jerk, she pulled him to his feet. "I'm going to put you to bed and then stay with you until you actually sleep. And that's final."

Clay wrapped a single arm around Alayna's waist, oddly needing the support to walk. He felt the others' eyes on him as Alayna led him to the second floor, back to the clean, quiet darkness of a hotel room. They collapsed together on the bed, wrapped in each other's arms, with Clay's brain finally allowing him a few moments of peace.

55.

Clay awoke hours later, with the warm sunlight streaming across his face, his arms, his naked abdomen. For a long moment, he wasn't entirely sure where he was: it could have been any hotel room in the world.

He rose from bed, his eyes glazed, as memories of the previous few days came back, images of Sam and Alex and the destroyed hotel reception desk flickering through his mind. "Jesus," he muttered, massaging his face with chapped hands. "Maia. I'm coming, baby. As soon as I can."

Alayna was nowhere in sight. Remembering his craving for a cup of coffee, Clay dressed quickly and headed out into the hotel. He was no longer surprised at his muscular development, even though he felt stronger than he had ever before. He flexed slightly, thinking back to the year he'd spent at the gym in his early thirties, trying to regain the strength he'd lost from his youth. Not even five days of rigorous training a week could fix him up. "You just like French fries too much," Valerie had teased him. "Is that such a crime?" he'd asked in reply.

Now, he was more muscle than anything else.

Downstairs, Clay entered the kitchen to find Sam inside, trying to light a can of sterno. She eyed

Clay, embarrassed, her cheeks turning pink. Shrugging, she gestured with the can.

"If only I could get this sucker lit, we could have a damn fine cup of coffee," she said sheepishly.

Clay leaned over, pulling a box of matchsticks from a drawer. He chose one with a long burn area, struck it, and then held it over the gel. After a long second, the can began to glow blue. Success.

"If only I'd known," Sam said, grinning slightly. "You're looking refreshed, by the way. Feeling better?"

"Physically, better than ever," Clay said, watching as she adjusted the sterno under the pot of water. "And I'm glad I found you. You're exactly the person I want to talk to."

"I thought you'd say that," Sam said, her eyes flickering away.

"You know Malcolm," he said.

"I do," Sam whispered, resigned to the conversation.

"Anything you can tell me about him. Whatever makes him tic . . . I'll take it. I'm going after him," Clay said, analyzing her face.

Sam leaned against the counter, considering his words. "You asked me yesterday what my plans are, Clay. And I told you I didn't know," she said. "That is, I didn't know until Alex woke up and I realized who he was."

"Malcolm's son?" Clay asked.

"I'm going with you," Sam said. "You're going to need my help with this one. And Malcolm and I, well . . . we have something of a history. A horrible history. That bastard has hurt me, and he's not going to hurt anyone else. Least of all you and definitely not your daughter." She leaned closer to Clay, almost spitting with anger. "I want revenge on that bastard just as much as you want your daughter back. And if we can go at him as a united front, we stand a better chance of succeeding."

Clay crossed his arms over his chest, giving Sam an exultant grin. The water began to bubble. The sound was warm, soothing and familiar in his ears. The two leaders regarded each other with respect. They were about to face a monster. A human monster, and they wouldn't hold anything back.

"That, Samantha, is the best news. It's the best news I've heard in a long damn time."

ABOUT THE AUTHOR

Paul B Kohler is the Amazon Bestselling Author of Linear Shift author, as well as the highly-acclaimed novel, The Hunted Assassin. His remarkable novel series, The Borrowed Souls is also gaining traction with its readers. Aside from his longer works, a number of his short stories have been included in various anthologies. His latest short, Rememorations, has been included in The Immortality Chronicles - a Top 5 SF Anthology and Hot New Releases. Rememorations was also nominated for Best American Science Fiction.

When not practicing architecture, Paul works on his writing. He lives in Littleton, Colorado.

To learn more about him and his books, visit www.PaulKohler.net

Made in the USA
Columbia, SC
30 January 2024

31060700R00157